# the day
# we are
# born

# the day we are born

## AN ELEMENTS NOVEL

# philippa cameron

The Day We Are Born

Copyright © Philippa Cameron 2014

Cover and interior design by Morgan Media

This is a work of fiction. Names, places, characters and incidents are either the product of the author's imagination or, if real, used fictitiously.

ISBN Print: 978-0-620-61906-6
ISBN E-book: 978-0-620-61377-4

*For my mom.*

*Wish you were here.*

*Friday*

# one

Today is a bad day.

I know this because when I wake up, everything's in brown and white. Sepia-colored. Like those old pictures in museums, or photographs of your great-grandmother. Nowadays people make their photos brown and white because they think it looks cool.

I think it looks like a bad day.

Then I hear my mom's voice.

"Elle? It's time to get up."

So I get up.

And I get going.

And I keep moving.

Keep moving.

Keep moving.

# two

My mother drops me off at the parking lot. I look up at the high-school building; at some point a facade was added to the drab seventies entrance in an attempt to update it, a wave of polycarbonate that looms over the students this morning. With a deep breath, I wade up the stairs and into my home room.

Libby's already there. She's got headphones on, the big clumpy kind that you wear over your head, and they dwarf her face. I slump into the seat next to her but she's not startled; she looks at me and then pulls down her headphones so they straddle her neck. I can hear a tinny beat coming from them.

"Bad day," she says.

It's not a question, but I nod anyway.

"Okay," she says. "That's enough about you. I think I've found the perfect song for your funeral, dude. Oh, I guess then it is still about you."

She sighs, a long exaggerated sigh. "Why is

everything about you? Who died and made you king of everything? Don't answer that," she says, even though I make no move to do or say anything. "Listen to this."

She pulls off the headphones, leans forwards and snaps them, quite painfully, over my ears. The sound is turned up really loudly so it takes a moment before I can focus on the music and then zoom into the lyrics. The words are incomprehensible at first; the singer is rolling them around in her mouth—or is it his mouth?—and then spitting them out. Suddenly, for a second, everything goes quiet, then, "I'm going straight to hell!" the falsetto voice shrieks. "And ya'll be right behind me!"

Libby's looking at me expectantly. "What do you think?" she mouths.

I pull off the headphones and shove them back at her.

"That," I say, "is the worst song ever."

"Isn't it?" says Libby. "It's so perfect."

I can't help but give a small half-smile at this. "Perfect? For my funeral? Are you completely insane?"

"Don't be ridiculous. You know I'm only partially insane. Besides, you're the one who's always saying that you're supposed to be dead."

I turn my head sharply but no one is close enough to hear what Libby just said.

She tilts her head. "Don't you want to go out with a kick-ass song? Oh wait," she says. "That's what I want. You'll probably want an *a capella* band at your funeral, singing The Carpenters love songs."

3

I throw a punch and connect with her upper arm. Luckily I don't know how to throw a punch, so she doesn't even wince. I stretch out my arms and crick my neck. I'm starting to feel better. Well, a little bit. Either the meds have started to kick in or Libby's version of therapy is working. Libby can tell, too, and raises her hand. We high five—ironically, of course. High-fiving may have made a comeback in this retrospective time in which we live, but only when done ironically. An ironic high-five looks like a regular high-five but if you raise an eyebrow—or, in Libby's case, perform an exaggerated wink to make up for a genetic deficiency in the single eyebrow-raising arena—it turns it into a post-modern, satirical and sarcastic gesture. Or, like, whatever.

After home room, it's a double period and Libby's not with me, so by the time the bell rings, I feel as if I'm drowning again. It takes all my energy to simply pack up my bag.

But I keep moving,

moving,

moving.

I've got my earbuds in and my iPod on—turned up loud—and I'm concentrating on the music that's filling all the gaps in my brain; gaps that are threatening to expand and snap the threads holding me together. So the only reason why I register that it's Sam di Rossi who's walking towards me is that I notice he's stepping in time to the beat in my head.

I pause to watch. His head is turned slightly and he's talking to a friend; I can see his mouth moving and it's

4

almost like he's singing the song I'm listening to. When he's nearly upon me, his rhythm changes as he sidesteps me. His arm skims mine as he passes. I start to walk again, but something in the air makes me turn back. Sam has stopped and he's staring at me, rubbing the place where our arms touched. The song ends, and in the hiatus before the next track I hear, "Elle?" Then the music starts up, students stream between us, and I walk away.

I get through the next class in one piece. Well, I seem like I'm in one piece from the outside. Inside, I'm a million slices of nerves and anxiety and loneliness and helplessness. I can't concentrate on what the teacher is saying; it's like I'm underwater so her words are damp and muffled. At one point she asks a question that I don't quite get and she's considering all the students in the class, looking for the answer, and I'm thinking,

don't ask me,

don't ask me,

don't ask me.

It's only when she points to a boy near me that I realize I've been holding my breath. I try to focus but I'm all over the place. And for some reason my thoughts keep going back to Sam. Our paths don't cross much anymore, and I'd almost forgotten him.

Almost.

My next class is a free period, thank god. Libby's waiting for me in the library, and as I sit down, she points her chin in the direction of a table surrounded by boys and girls.

"Speaking about big breasts…"

"I didn't know we were speaking about big breasts," I say.

"… I freaking hate that Sydney chick."

Sydney's sitting at the head of the table, and everyone is leaning in her direction. She's obviously telling a story and her audience is enthralled. She reaches the punchline and there's muted laughter.

"She's not that bad," I say. "She can't help being that hot."

"That's not why I hate her. She's so freaking stupid. Can't she see that the only reason why she's so popular is because of the way she looks?"

"I didn't know being popular was important to you," I say, getting an evil glare in return. "And she's not that stupid."

"Wanna bet? Yesterday, Mr Gatter asked the class what you call the clowns who entertained the kings and queens during the Middle Ages, and she stuck up her hand and said, in all seriousness, 'Lepers.' "

I snort out loud—I'm still feeling too overwhelmed to laugh—turning all the heads at the opposite table. I duck down.

"I would love to be her," I say quietly. "Beautiful and dumb. She's never going to have any problems in life. Everyone will always want to help her because she's gorgeous, and she won't worry about anything because she's too dumb to understand that anything is ever wrong."

I glance over at Sydney. "She never has to think."

I grimace. "I'm so tired of thinking."

This time I'm the one that gets punched. And Libby has incredible upper body strength and I groan in pain.

"Let's get out of here," says Libby, putting her bag on her lap. "History class, James, and don't spare the horses."

I take the handles of her wheelchair. "Let's roll," I say, and I wheel her out.

# three

About a year ago, I was at a football match with Julie, who was sort of my best friend, and Libby and Savannah, who were also sort of best friends. (If Libby heard me calling anyone her best friend, she'd rip my heart out and barbecue it for lunch.)

At the time, we were all caught up in a whirlpool of hormones and tests and boyfriends and acne and shopping and movies, when Libby and I found ourselves being pulled out by the same current.

For me, I was giving up. I tried to fake it, but it took up too much energy, and I needed all I had to simply get by.

For Libby, it was different because she'd never give up. But being confined to a wheelchair never let her be ordinary so, instead, she made a decision to be extraordinary.

Thanks to Libby and her wheelchair, a group of us had prime seats on the corner of the football field, close to the action but tucked out of sight. And I was having a good day.

Someone was passing around wine coolers and beers. I'm not a good drunk. It's not like I drink very often but when I do, it's not a pretty sight. I've read the package inserts of my medication and they make it perfectly clear that they do not mix with alcohol, but what can I say? I'm a stupid teenager. My bad days on a hangover transmogrify into bad days with a twist—I can't sleep and I have panic attacks. Funnily enough, my *really* bad days aren't affected by hangovers. It's as if they're so bad already that nothing can touch them.

Coffee sometimes has a similar effect, especially if I drink it in the evening. Bad night. And then a bad day. My mom's got me into tea, though, and I can live with only one cup of coffee a day. And I can live without alcohol. But every now and then, having a few drinks helps me let go, just for a couple of hours. Of course, I'm punished the next day but I can handle it. Maybe because I realize that it's self-induced, so I wallow in it. My mom would throw a fit if she knew that I indulged every now and then, and not a fit like a regular parent would throw if their regular teenager drank. I mean a holy cow, out-of-this-world hissy fit if she knew that I was self-sabotaging—a term that we've both come across in the literature she's gathered. She's made it very clear to me that she is so proud of the way that I handle myself; I don't think it crosses her mind that sometimes I might be causing my bad days myself.

But it's rare that I do. This was one of those rare times.

I was sitting next to Libby and we'd both had a couple of wine coolers (or three or four) and I was feeling very chilled. One of the girls in our party had clearly had several more than a couple—she was being seriously obnoxious, and if that wasn't enough, she started a high-pitched shrieking in support of our team. Then right in front of us, she slipped and fell, smearing mud all over her jeans and her hideously tie-dyed shirt. As she dropped to the ground, I burst out laughing. I couldn't help myself. I have this thing about people who fall over: I find it hysterical. I know, I know, it's really childish, but there you have it. The girl looked at me in anger as she picked herself up and stalked off. I realized that Libby was examining me, and then she started chuckling.

"Thank the freak she's going," Libby said.

"Absolutely," I said. "I couldn't hear myself think."

"No volume control on that dude."

"No," I said. "The problem was her shirt."

Libby looked at me, puzzled.

"Her shirt," I said. "So loud."

She gave me a half grin. "Funny."

She yelled after the girl. "Hey, Trudy! There's a phone call for you. It's the seventies. They want their shirt back."

I laughed. And I don't know what came over me— too many wine coolers, I guess—but I suddenly blurted out, "Libby. What's it like? Being in a wheelchair, I mean?"

I already knew what had happened to her:

a pony outride on a family holiday when she was ten,

a spooked horse,

a bad fall,

an injury to the spinal cord,

a wheelchair.

I didn't know her before then—her family moved here because there's a rehab center nearby—but according to legend, she was as much a bad-ass then as she is now. I don't know what she went through in her initial stages of rehab but I do know it must have been hard. She still spends three afternoons a week at the center where she works out and gets her legs massaged. There are also loads of serious problems that can crop up when you're a paraplegic but these are something Libby won't talk about.

"Oh, you know," she told me then, in a sing-song voice. "I have a leg catheter for my urine. I self-stimulate my bowels first thing in the morning so I don't need to take a crap for the rest of the day."

I already knew all this. Everyone does. We had a talk from our Health teacher when Libby first arrived at school, and I also know that she's had an accident once or twice during classes, but with Libby's screw-you attitude, these occasions are seen as taboo.

I know it must kill her, though.

"Uh," I said. "I mean..."

"I know what you mean," she said, coldly. But then

she rolled her eyes.

"It's kind of cool. I mean, I never get tired from standing. I never have to find a seat. My parents get to park right outside the entrance to the mall. And I always get to sit in the front at movies and concerts and football matches.

"What I hate," she says, her voice going cold again, "is the sympathy. The freaking sympathy. Everyone sorry for the poor, little disabled kid. And another thing…"

She didn't even seem to pause for breath.

"…everyone thinks all disabled people are so brave. And so strong. And so accepting of their disability. Well, I'm not accepting it, and while I am the bravest and strongest person I know, it's not because I'm disabled, it's because I'm a freaking machine and always have been."

She only stopped now to take another swig from her bottle, and then she smacked her fist down on her armrest.

"I refuse to be some stereotype."

Smack. Swig.

"I don't want to be part of this freak show."

Smack. Swig.

"I will not be the poster girl for the disabled."

Smack. Swig.

Then she emptied the rest of her bottle down her throat in one go. I wasn't sure if I was supposed to say something here, but Libby hadn't finished. "And I hate other people staring. Just after I'd had the accident, everywhere I'd go, I'd read their thoughts: What an awful thing for such a pretty little girl—stuck in a wheelchair all her life. Like if I was butt-ugly, what would they think then? Oh, that's okay, she wasn't going to get anywhere in life with those looks anyway."

Because the thing is, Libby is hot. Like the most gorgeous girl you have ever seen. That kind of hot. She tries to disguise it, of course. Her ice-blonde hair is dyed pitch black and cut jaggedly along her jawline. She goes for weeks without washing it, and usually clumps it around her head with bobby pins. So as not to be confused with the Goths, she doesn't wear a stitch of make-up. Of course, this doesn't make any difference. The dark hair turns her skin ivory, brings out the brilliant blue of her eyes and casts a shadow on her high, perfectly symmetrical cheekbones. She's still hot. But I'd never tell her this.

And that's probably one of the reasons I like to be around her—although I'd never tell her this, either—because next to her, I fade into the background with my

brown hair,

brown eyes,

brown skin.

In my uniform of jeans and T-shirts and sneakers, I'm just the girl who pushes Libby's wheelchair.

After her tirade and downing of drinks, we managed to make it to the bathroom before she threw up. She only paused between retches to lash out: "And if you tell anybody what I've told you, dude, I'll kill you."

So I decided to give her something in return.

Sitting on the floor in the bathroom, I said, "Well, if you kill me, you'd kind of be doing me a favor."

That got her attention. She wiped her mouth with a paper towel and said, "What the hell is that supposed to mean?"

"It's like this," I said, carefully. "I think I'm supposed to be dead. Or I'm not supposed to be alive. I don't know if there's a difference between those two things, but either way, I'm not meant to be here."

Libby was silent, for once, I guess trying to figure out exactly what I was saying.

"I don't want to kill myself or anything stupid like that," I said quickly, in case that's what she was thinking. "I'm just so tired of *being*. Like you know when you're tired at school and you want to go home? It's like that all the time for me; that I want to go home. Even when I am home."

I stopped. Libby still didn't say anything. I wanted her to say something.

"Does this make any sense?" I asked.

She nodded eventually.

"Perfect sense," she said. "You have this life. But you don't want it. You don't feel like you're supposed to be here. Just like I have this freaking life that I don't want. And I don't want to be in this chair. Who's to say who's more crippled—you or me? Your mind or my legs? We're both broken."

She got it. She got me. I remember holding my breath. I wanted to cry. But I knew Libby wasn't a cry-on-your-shoulder kind of girl. So I went the other way.

"Jeez, that's deep, Libby," I said. But I couldn't meet her eyes.

"What can I say?" she threw back. "Still waters run deep. Not that I'm ever going to run anywhere."

My afternoon of drinking resulted in two bad days in a row, but once I'd come through the darkness, I knew it had been worth it. I had found someone who got me.

At school the next week, I saw Libby waiting at the bus stop next to the school parking lot. My mother was due to pick me up in five minutes—she drops me off and fetches me every day, like I'm in elementary school. And I let her; it's her way of trying to protect me, even though I don't really know what she's trying to protect me from.

Mostly myself, I guess.

Libby was ramping her wheelchair up and down the edge of the sidewalk.

"Are you waiting for your mom?" I asked.

She rolled her eyes.

"I should be so lucky. My mother," she said, drawing out the name, "doesn't believe that I'm disabled. She doesn't believe that not being able to walk is a disability. And, as such, she doesn't believe that I should be treated like a disabled person. So I have to catch the bus to and from school."

She wheeled her chair viciously into the sidewalk and spun around.

"But the bus with ramp facilities for disabled people—though why I would need these facilities since I'm clearly not disabled—only comes at five, so I'm stuck at school until then every day.

"And did I mention that in the morning, the bus—and again, there's only one morning bus with a ramp—arrives promptly at seven, so I have to be up at the crack of dawn every day."

Another violent crash into the concrete.

"And," another crash, "my parents won't get me an electric wheelchair. 'You have to do it for yourself,' they say. 'It's good for your upper-body strength,' they say.' "

Crash.

That didn't sound cool. But I thought I'd try and one-up her.

"You think you've got it bad," I said, looking down at my watch. "Wait for it. Wait for it."

"What the hell am I waiting for?"

"Wait for it..."

I was still bent over my watch, and as the hand twitched onto the four, I snapped my fingers.

"And she's here."

Libby started as a car curved around the corner. "Jeez, how did you do that?"

"My mother picks me up every day. Every day. At exactly 4 o'clock. Every day."

"Dude, that's insane," she said. "How old are you, anyway? Eight?"

My mom was right in front of us now, grinning through the windshield in that way that crinkles up her nose. I decided to try something.

"So. Do you want a lift, or what?" I asked. "The trunk is big enough to take that fancy chair of yours."

I blushed. It wasn't like me to be that cocky. And even after our bonding session at football, I was still wary of her. I knew I was taking a risk.

Libby raised her eyebrows.

"Oh yeah? So that's how it is," she said. "In that case, dude, I hope you've been pushing weights, because you're going to have to get used to picking me up."

My friendship with Libby is easy. I find the idea of being among a big group of friends exhausting. Yeah, she's rude, cold, callous, sometimes cruel, often mean. And yet, she's exactly what I need. For the first time, I found someone who doesn't take any effort to be friends with.

I can't do effort.

# four

So I get through the rest of the day, buoyed up by Libby, but we're not in the same last class, and I'm exhausted by the time the final bell goes. I'm tempted to call my mom to come and fetch me early, but I know this worries her. I've got drama club this afternoon, something I usually love, but today, I don't love anything.

Libby proves me wrong.

You can never miss Libby coming down the hallway—and it's not because she's in a wheelchair; it's because of the yelps of pain as she careens into the ankles in front of her.

"Elle!" she shrieks. "You won't freaking believe it! You won't! You won't!"

As she reaches me, she picks up the phone lying on her lap and tosses it to me. I only just manage to catch it, and I scowl at her. I can't do this now—this Libby enthusiasm—and suddenly, I want to cry. But Libby's not picking up on any of the cues.

"Read it, dude. Read what's on my phone."

"Libby…"

"Freaking read it!"

So I read it. Then I look at Libby, annoyed.

"Yes, Libby, we already know they're coming here. But only on two dates at concerts on the opposite sides of the country. Are you trying to torture me again?"

"You freak!" Libby yells, making several students whimper away from her. "Read the whole freaking thing!"

I don't get it the first time—the brown mist in front of my eyes is staining the words, but then they filter through. There's a news flash at the bottom of the page—and it's literally flashing.

"New date added. December 16. Fort Nottingham Festival."

Fort Nottingham. That's less than 300 miles from here. I'd heard of this music festival—mostly underground punk rock and death metal so not quite my style, but Besiegung would be there! Besiegung—my favorite band in the whole universe—is coming here! Next week!

My world is still in brown and white, but not even that can stop the warmth that flushes through my system. Libby and I lock eyes.

"Oh my god," I say. "We're going to watch Besiegung. Live. In concert. On Friday."

"Still want to be dead?" asks Libby.

"Yes," I say, sadly, then in a burst of joy, "but not until I've seen Besiegung live!"

I know, that's not funny. But sometimes, when I'm like this, that's the only sort of thing that can make me laugh.

Libby's into music in a big way. She's got pretty loose morals when it comes to most things in life, except music. She's non-negotiable on piracy. You do it, you die. She runs a website where you can out people who you know are illegally downloading or copying music. It's called be-the-rat.com.

Her tastes run across the spectrum:

classical,

country,

rock 'n' roll,

just plain rock,

jazz,

ska,

seventies punk,

eighties punk,

post-punk.

And many others in between. But she has a special place in her heart for neo-punk. Specifically German. And that's how she found Besiegung—someone outed a

German friend for copying their music; she'd never heard of Besiegung so she (legally) downloaded one of their songs. And fell hard.

I'm more into local rock, but there was something about Besiegung that struck a chord. It was partly their sound—anguished and groaning, and partly their lyrics—anguished and groaning, and partly because of the lead singer—anguished and groaning and gorgeous.

We're possibly a little obsessed with the band. We have found translations for all their songs, but we've also become pretty fluent in German. Of course, when I mean pretty fluent, I actually mean pretty fluent for lustful teens who really only want to learn how to say, "I want to have your baby" in German.

We took an online course in German last summer, discovering loads of English words that we have stolen from German. One of my favorite German-English words is "angst", which means when you're filled with anxiety or dread, usually with no real reason behind it. It's an accurate description of how I am some of the time. It was nice to come across one word that can sum up what I'm full of on a bad day. I haven't yet found one that fits my *really* bad days, though.

But mostly, I call it like it is.

Hi, my name is Elle, and I am depressed.

Now that's a funny word. Depressed. To press down. I don't think it's the right word to characterize the condition, however, as it's got way too many connotations attached to it and you get judged by it. You're depressed? Verdict—there's something wrong with you. People often link depression and sadness together, for example. I am sad, and often, but I'm not always sad. Sometimes I'm happy, and other times I'm really, really happy. I can still feel joy and I can still laugh. I don't walk around with a black cloud hanging over my head and a surly expression on my face.

There's an old English word for depression: grevoushede. I don't know exactly what it means, but I think the first part means grief. And that's probably the closest way of explaining what happens to me on my *really* bad days. I am grieving.

What I do find interesting about the word "depressed" is that it stays the same no matter what tense it's in.

I was depressed.

I am depressed.

I will be depressed.

It doesn't matter which way you look at it, you're always depressed.

Libby's spinning her chair around and students are scattering like skittles.

"Töte das Biest!" she bellows. "Töte das Biest!"

This is the title of Besiegung's latest single.

Töte das Biest.

Kill the Beast.

Rumoured to be named after the boys' ranting, "Kill the beast!" in Lord of the Flies, naturally Libby now has an encyclopaedic knowledge of the novel. If you ask her about it, this is what you'll hear: "It's an allegory about man's true desires. We don't want civilization, we want savagery; not order, but chaos. It's about man's innate need for power, and what he will do to get it."

Seriously, ask her. That's word for word what she'll tell you.

"Komm, Freundin," says Libby. "Wir haben jetzt Pläne zu machen."

She's right. We do have plans to make. The most important one being how the hell I'm going to convince my mother to let me go to the festival. When I read the date of the concert, December 16, something clicked in my brain, but I only place it now. It isn't that it's a Friday—school's closing for the Christmas break so the timing is perfect. But the problem is that the 16th is *next* Friday: Stephen Lawd's memorial service in the city.

My mom knew Stephen when she used to live in London. In fact, I have a sneaky suspicion that they were dating before my dad arrived on the scene. In any case, they always kept in touch and later Stephen spent five years over here working on the same projects as my mother. He returned to London years ago, but they were always in the same orbit, so their lives connected again and again. It was a sudden heart attack that took his life two weeks ago, and my mom was the one organizing the memorial service for his American colleagues and friends.

Besiegung is playing just before lunchtime on Friday, so we would have to leave in the early hours of the

23

morning to get there on time. Ordinarily, my mom would have leapt to volunteer to make the eight-hour round-trip to Fort Nottingham. But this Friday, both she and my dad will be in the city all day, and the likelihood of my parents letting me go to the festival with anyone else is slim. Because although I'm 16 and most 16-year-olds would probably be allowed to go, I'm not your typical 16-year-old.

"How close was she to this dead dude?" asks Libby after I tell her.

"Libby."

"Okay, okay. So what's plan B?"

"What about your mom?" Libby's mother is the one of the few adults that I know my mom is happy for me to be driven around by. But as I ask this, I already know the answer.

Libby's mom is great. Both her parents are. They changed their lives to accommodate their daughter— their only child—and it's taken an emotional and financial toll on them. I'm not sure, though, if I agree with their strategy towards helping Libby become totally independent of them, and recently this backfired. To punish her parents for making her take the bus every day—even though most afternoons she comes home with me—she's pushed the boundaries of her freedom to the limits and beyond. This past weekend was the last straw. She'd gone to watch a play at the Roundhouse Theatre as part of a school excursion. I was having a *really* bad day so I wasn't with her. It was the final night and Libby decided to stay for the afterparty. She arrived home in the early hours of the next morning, drunk and—somehow, despite the clear weather conditions—soaking wet.

So she's grounded.

But that's not the problem—Libby's always getting into some sort of trouble and managing to get out of it. I'm one hundred percent sure that she'll be able to convince her parents to let her go to Besiegung—they know how crazy she is about the band. But driving us on a 600-mile round trip—on that point, I'm not so sure.

Libby is sure.

"Not a chance in hell that my parents will drive us," she says. "They were really pissed last weekend. Not pissed enough to not let me go. But pissed enough to make it as difficult as possible for me. I mean, even if I wasn't in trouble, they'd probably tell me I had to make my own way there. I'll try anyway, but don't hold your breath."

I'm pushing Libby down the hall now and I realize she's texting as we're going.

"Libby," I tell her. "Get off your phone. You know the policy."

"Oh, please," she scoffs. "Who's going to tell the poor crippled girl to get off the phone?"

"Who're you texting anyway?"

"Julie and Savannah. We need an emergency meeting to decide how the freaking hell we're going to get to Fort Nottingham."

When Libby and I started hanging around last year,

Julie and Savannah quietly hooked up—purely in the friendship sense. There was a bit of awkwardness at first, but we all got over it, and Savannah, in particular, seemed relieved to have moved in a different direction from Libby. From my side, Julie was a bit of a high-maintenance friend, but now the pressure was off and I could enjoy her company without the drama that she loves to dwell in.

Julie and Savannah are the only ones who are occasionally permitted to join Team Libby. Libby finds it hard to get on with anyone who… well, actually anyone, period. I think Libby humors the others for my sake; she'd be happy with only the two of us. But she knows that sometimes there's strength in numbers. Like now.

"Sav's got her license," she says.

"She only got it last month," I say. "No way her mom's going to let her take the car."

Let's not even go there on how my mom would never let me ride in a car with someone who only had their license for a month. Especially someone who wasn't an adult or a member of our family.

Oh, wait. "What about my brother?" I say.

"But he's in the city?"

"He'd come out for this. For me. His favorite little sister."

"And his favorite big sister?"

"No, Sylvia's heading for the West Coast next week for work—I'm seeing her tomorrow when she comes over to say goodbye. But Johnny might be around."

26

"Won't he be out saving the walruses or something?"

"Or something. But I'm sure he'd be game. In fact, he'd probably enjoy it."

Libby starts texting again. "Just cancelling our pow-wow. Let's get the lowdown on your brother first before we bring the other two into it."

"Libby," I say.

"Oh, fine. I'll still tell them about the festival. But you'll have to babysit them if they come with."

She spins her chair and wheelies as we enter the drama club classroom.

"Töte das Biest!" she yells.

# five

"How did it go with your parents?" I ask.

It's evening and I'm lying in bed and I'm on the phone with Libby.

"Not as well as I expected," she says.

"What? What do you mean?"

This is bad, very bad. If Libby's parents won't let her go, then we're done for.

"They're really pissed with me, dude. So uncool. I mean, what did I do this time that was any different to every other time? And if they want me to be independent, why would they then try and clip my wings? Parents—ugh—they're so inconsistent. At least I'm consistently bad so there are no surprises. But when I mentioned that Besiegung were playing on Friday, they lectured me for, like, over an hour. Responsibility this, freaking boundaries that."

I'm taking deep breaths now, one of the techniques I use to help me when I start feeling out of control.

Libby's still ranting about her parents, but her voice has been dampened and I'm focusing on my breathing. I'm coming up for air when I hear her say, "So there's no way in hell that they're going to take us."

While I'm processing this, Libby continues, "So I guess it's plan B then, or C or D or whatever we're on now."

"You mean they're still letting you go?" I exhale.

"Of course," she says. "That was never in question. If I thought it was, I wouldn't have told them and snuck out anyway."

Okay, we're still okay. One hurdle overcome. Now it's only the small matter of the towering mountain that is my parents. Usually, their presence in my life is steadfast and durable; right now, I'd like it to be a little more pliable.

"Okay," says Libby, "so there's that limo hire service. How cool would it be to pitch up at the concert in a limo? Or I think there's a bus we can catch to Kennicott. From there, it's only a hundred miles to Fort Nottingham. You hide in the bushes and I'll hitch; no one's going to drive past a poor cripple."

But I know at this point it's Johnny or nothing. So does Libby.

"It's all on you, Elle," Libby says to me.

"So, no pressure, then."

But she's already gone.

I turn on my music system and stretch out on my bed. It's only nine o'clock but I'm tired. I had felt on an even keel by the time my mom picked me up today;

even if I hadn't really been aware of my change in mood, I could see it reflected in the relief on her face as I got into the car. It lasted well into the evening; then, as the sky darkened, so did I.

I'd taken my herbal sleeping capsule and two anti-anxiety tablets before I phoned Libby, but they haven't taken effect yet so I'm finding it difficult to breathe. I concentrate on inhaling and exhaling—actually picturing my lungs expanding and contracting—and this seems to help. I'll fall asleep with my music still playing; I'm too scared to do it in silence because I'll be alone with my thoughts.

So I'm lying on my bed, listening to myself breathe through the music. And, finally, sleep comes.

Saturday

# six

Today is a bad day.

I know it before I even open my eyes. My dream is still hovering, even though I'm awake. I'm being chased and I'm

running,

running,

running.

There's someone else with me, and I'm helping them to

run,

run,

run.

Everywhere we go, every turn we take, there's an obstacle in our path, but we keep on running.

This is not a new dream; each time the setting is different and the person I'm helping is different although I never know who they are, but everything else is the same. Especially the feeling of hopelessness.

I've Googled my dream and all the sites I've read say the same thing: What you dream is paralleled with what's happening in your waking life. So what am I running from? My life? My death?

What I couldn't find out is why there's a big part of dream-me that wants to stop running and be caught.

I open my eyes. Sepia. I try to focus on the poster of Besiegung on the wall. I hum a bar from Töte das Biest. Then I remember that it's Saturday. Thank god. I wouldn't have made it through another school day. I hum a bit more—this always helps. My bedroom door is slightly open and I can hear voices downstairs in the kitchen—small islands of words that only join together when I concentrate on them.

One voice is my mom's. She's saying, "It wasn't a good day. Five good days, but now back to this."

The other voice is my sister's, Sylvia. "I thought the medication would be working again by now."

Mom: "I did too. And I guess it is—five good days in a row is unusual. But my heart sank when I saw her yesterday morning."

Sylvia: "Maybe it's too soon. She hasn't been back on these very long. Maybe it takes a while for the meds to settle in again and work consistently."

Mom: "You're right. I'm venting. I'm just …"

Sylvia: "Scared."

Both voices go silent. I remember why Sylvia is here—we're going out for brunch, only the two of us, a ritual of ours every month. It's going to be hard, but I have to get up. So I hum.

And I get up.
And I get going.
And I keep moving.
Keep moving.
Keep moving.

# seven

~~

When I get out of the shower, Sylvia's sitting on my bed and she hands me a cup of tea.

"Morning, sunshine," she says.

I'm happy to see her—really, I am—but if she wasn't here, I would have sunk back under my covers and not come out again until... until...

"So get dressed, lazy," she says, "and let's hit the road—I'm starving! And the sun's out—well, a little. So you can throw on a pretty dress for a change instead of jeans."

She sees my face. "No? Pity. I'd kill for your legs."

Sylvia's always been a bit bossy, or maybe it seems this way since she's 16 years older than me. My brother, Johnny, is a year older than Sylvia. Which clearly makes me the youngest child in the family. Youngest by a long way. They're both named after members of my mom's family that she left behind: Sylvia for her sister and John for her father.

My mom is South African. During the eighties, she became an anti-apartheid activist when she was at university and took advantage of having a British mother and a British passport by taking the cause to London. It was during one of the protests outside South Africa House in Trafalgar Square that she met my American father. He had taken a year off from his studies to backpack through Europe, and was on the last leg of his trip in England. He was photographing the Trafalgar lions when he got caught in the current created by the demonstrators. My mother linked his arm through hers without even seeing who it was, and soon he was joining in the chants of 'Free Mandela!' Afterwards, at a party in a nearby pub, he fell in love with her over a pint, and extended his stay until she fell in love with him too.

They found themselves without a common country. My mother desperately wanted to return home to South Africa where the African National Congress had recently been unbanned, and there was talk of Nelson Mandela being released from prison. She had to be there. My father had been accepted for a post-graduate degree at MIT and was expected on campus in a month's time. As my mother waited to board her plane at Heathrow, heading for Johannesburg, my father broke down and begged her to stay. She didn't. But she spent the entire flight composing a letter to him, which she mailed as soon as she landed.

"I will come to you in five years," the letter said. "If you still want me, I will be yours."

There was a lot more in the letter, which I've read countless times. In fact, I have my own copy—the original is framed and hung over my parents' bed. The letter was a stream of consciousness, an outpouring of love and grief and fear and joy. It was a declaration, a promise, a hope. And my father's reply was in a brief aerogram.

"I will wait for you."

Five years, however, turned out to be too long to wait. My father met and married someone else before the third year was up. It's a tale that always gets a laugh at parties, especially when my mother tells it with a particularly injured and aghast expression on her face. After a letter like that, how could anyone not have waited? But the story has a happy ending, of course— happy, that is, for my parents. My father's starter marriage didn't last more than a year. My mother got to vote in the first-ever democratic elections in South Africa, then applied for and got an internship at the African Department of the University of Washington. Five years and two months to the day of her leaving my father, she returned to him.

My brother's arrival less than a year into their reunion led them to marriage. My mother even took my dad's last name, Marshall, even though she'd always sworn she'd keep her own. Eighteen months later they completed their pigeon pair with Sylvia, and considered their family complete.

Johnny had just finished high school when my mother's stomach flu turned into a pregnancy. My father disappeared for the whole night when he found out, returning in the early hours of the morning with whiskey on his breath and a bag of diapers in his hands from the all-night convenience store. It was the only time he hesitated, reported my mother. From then on, he surrounded her like an atoll protecting a lagoon. He bought books on pregnancy and birth as if he and my mother were first-time parents, and the contents of the fridge started mimicking an organic health store. He joined a gym to lose the five pounds that had wrapped themselves around his waist in the past 10 years. He insisted that my brother and sister join them at the pre-natal classes in case he wasn't around when my mom went into labor. My mom was in her forties, so there were risks involved, but according to my family members—all of whom were at the birth—I was perfect.

My full name is Elaine but everyone calls me Elle. Which is pronounced like the letter 'L' and not like Ellie the elephant. I am named after my South African grandmother. Apparently the name fits as everyone says I look just like her. I often wish she was still alive so I could ask her what she was like as a teenager. If she was like me.

# eight

"What were you like as a teenager?" I ask.

Sylvia and I are at a coffee shop on Ridge Avenue, sitting at a table on the sidewalk. She's just commented on how blue the sky is today; to me, it's the color of a dull sunset. We're both eating bagels and while Sylvia's relishing hers, I'm struggling to get mine down.

"Oh god, I was horrible," says Sylvia, her tongue dabbing a spot of mayo from her lip. "I don't know how Mom and Dad put up with me. I turned 13 and turned into a monster."

She's laughing now at the look on my face. I love her laugh. She does that same scrunchy thing with her nose that my mom does, but her mouth is much wider and her laugh much louder. I glance at the couple sitting at the table next to us; they're smiling at Sylvia and her laugh.

"Seriously?" I say. "Miss Perfect?"

Sylvia's a lawyer. She tornadoed through law school,

gathering up accolades and awards as she went, picking up a sought-after job at a top law firm in the city before she'd even taken her last exam. And there was no sign of her momentum slowing down. No glass ceiling for her; it was pulled into her orbit and shattered.

"Look, I was always perfect," she says, her nose still scrunched up. "You just couldn't see my perfection under all the black clothing and black eye-liner and black attitude."

I had seen photos of Sylvia as a teen, and they were horrible, but I couldn't reconcile my sister of today with her awful teenager of yesterday.

"Poor Dad bore the brunt of it," Sylvia says to me. "I don't think I spoke to him for about two years. Nothing that he did or said was right in my eyes, and I thought he was embarrassing. And you know Dad; he never gave up trying, which made it worse. Luckily, he's forgiven me."

"What sort of things did you do?"

"Nothing too bad. The good girl was always below the surface. I think I needed to experiment with being the total opposite of what I was before. I'd stay out past my curfew—only ever an hour or so but as long as it wasn't on curfew. I dated that dreadful Robbie Smith; no one's seen him in years. He's probably in jail…

"And I smoked cigarettes. And pot once or twice. Mom caught me smoking—do you know what she said when she did?"

"Knowing Mom, something profound."

"I was sitting on the back porch with Robbie; Mom

41

arrived home early and found us there smoking. Without missing a beat, she said, 'If you can't beat 'em, join 'em', and took a cigarette out of Robbie's pack and lit up.''

"Really? Mom smoked?"

"She smoked a bit before she had Johnny and me, but hadn't in years. But her sitting there smoking took all the fun away from doing something illicit. I stumped out my cigarette and stormed off. But I never smoked again.''

I have never really thought about my mom's life before she had me. Or before she had the others. Or before she met my dad. It feels weird, imagining her as a girl, as a student, as a newly-wed, as a new mom. All I know about her is what she is now. And I also know that she wasn't like me when she was a teenager.

I'm drifting and then I realize that Sylvia is studying me, so I cut off a slice of my bagel and pop it in my mouth, even though I don't want it.

"Why do you want to know about my being a teenager?" she asks.

I swallow.

"I guess it's because, well, because of what I am. What *I'm* like as a teenager."

"So what else do you want to know?"

"Were you—are you—I mean, were you like me? Like this?"

"Like what?" Sylvia asks gently.

"You know. Having good days and bad days."

Sylvia leans back in her chair. I can tell she is

thinking about the right thing to say. I can tell she's trying to find the right words.

"I guess I was moody, and certainly sulky," she eventually says. "There's so much going on around you and within you when you're a teenager. So many changes."

It isn't enough. I want more.

"But were you like me?" I sound harsh. But I want the truth. And I get it.

"No," she says. "I wasn't like you. But," she leans in and squeezes my hand, "I don't know what like you is. Maybe it was there—it would certainly explain the moodiness, and there were definitely bad days."

"But not *really* bad days."

"No." She's gentle again. "Not really bad days."

I watch the road. A car comes around the corner and I wonder what it would be like if it hit me. If the driver had fought with his wife earlier and she'd threatened to leave him and he'd stormed out the house and was driving to who knows where to clear his head and he's furious and scared and thinking about what life would be like without her, and he takes the corner too fast and runs up the kerb and hits me, and I'm dead.

# nine

When I was old enough to realize that my siblings were much older than me, my mother sat me down and explained. In South Africa I would be called a *laat-lammetjie*, which, translated from its Afrikaans means "late lamb", a term South African farmers use to describe sheep that are born really late in the season. They're not unwelcome, my mother quickly reassured me, just the contrary. A surprise addition to the herd, which means more wealth for the farmer.

My dad has his own explanation for my arrival. We have this old table in the kitchen that my mom paints a new color every year. With scrapes and bumps, bits of the old paint show through. My dad says if you cut off one of the legs, you'd be able to see how old the table is by the rings of color, and catalogue its history: blue was first, chosen to match the kitchen cupboards that the house came with when my parents first bought it; purple was next—the kitchen had been overhauled in minimalist white and my mother said it needed brightening up; there's a hint of orange on one corner (even my mom agreed that had been a hideous mistake); and pale grey on another, signalling a moment— however short-lived—of maturity, said my sister. It was replaced the following year by sunshine yellow.

When I was about 10, it was aquamarine. It was a Sunday and both my siblings were home for the weekend. Sunday is always a family day in our house, with a roast on offer for lunch, a nod to my mother's South African upbringing. It isn't reserved for family members, however; there is usually an assortment of friends and colleagues at the table too.

This particular Sunday, it was only us for a change. I don't remember what it was that prompted me to begin a discussion of why I was born so late in their lives.

"Well," said my father. "There is a very good reason for that. You see, your mother and I didn't do a very good job with raising Sylvia and John. But after two children, we reckoned we were ready to become the perfect parents. So we had you so that we could correct the mistakes we made with your brother and sister."

"Dad!" said Sylvia, who was then about 26. "That's horrible! Are you trying to say that we were just your practise children?"

"If that's how you see it…."

My brother threw a napkin across the table at my dad.

"Actually," John said, "you guys were rather terrible parents."

My mom choked down a mouthful of peas, but before she could object, my brother had launched into a list of offences.

"Remember when Dad lost me in the mall?" (Longest 60 seconds of my life, my father always said, before a screaming toddler was deposited back into his arms by a disapproving shopkeeper.) "Or when he forgot to pick you"—a gesture in my sister's direction—"up from school and you thought it was a good idea to hitch home…"

"Or when Mom," Sylvia joined in, "let you stay over with some new boy from school when you were 14 without checking that there would be any parental supervision. When she collected you the next morning, you were still reeking of marijuana."

"Or when…"

"Okay, okay," laughed my mother. "You have proven your father's point."

"But you've done a pretty good job with Elle," said my brother, winking at me across the table.

"Oh, gee, thanks," said my dad.

"Although it was pretty creepy when Mom was pregnant."

"Sylvia Marshall!" said my mother.

"What do you mean, creepy?" I asked.

"It was awful," she said, and I held my breath. "I remember thinking that this meant that everyone would know that Mom and Dad were still…"

My dad made a grunting noise, and Sylvia broke off, grinning. I don't think I had started breathing again yet, and at only ten years old not understanding what she was trying to say, I was only focusing on the word 'awful'.

"I mean, I was almost 16. I was embarrassed that my elderly parents were having another child. And I was jealous. I was the baby of the family, and soon I wouldn't be anymore. I didn't want to lose the attention."

I was drowning now.

"But," she said, "when I saw you in hospital, I realised that I wouldn't trade anything for you. I fell in love with you instantly."

I took in a great gulp of air, and I knew my eyes were sparkling.

"Jeepers," said Johnny, "I hope none of your corporate clients ever get to see this gushy, sentimental side of you—they'd drop you in a second."

This time *he* got a napkin in the face.

Johnny's also a lawyer. But unlike Sylvia, law school wasn't a means to an end. He joined every group that he could in his first year:

Save the Seals,

Save the Whales,

Save the Children,

Save the Earth.

By the time he had finished with school—which took him a year longer than everybody else—he was chairperson of all these groups, and it was to no one's surprise that he ended up taking a position with an environmental non-profit that was attached to the college. And he's still there. His salary is pitiful, he says, but his heart is full.

So we all knew his words at the table were in jest; Johnny gets tears in his eyes when he watches any commercials with sad small children or animals, although of course he claims that it's his contacts making his eyes water.

Even though I was only ten, I still felt that something was missing in the story of how I got to be. That something was missing in me. Something that would explain all the grief I felt. So many things made me sad:

a rainy day,

the old lady in rags who pushed her trolley around the mall parking lot,

the girl in my class whose parents got divorced,

the posters on the wall outside the bakery of the dogs at the shelter that needed homes.

And Sunday nights.

# ten

I don't know what it was about Sunday nights when I was younger. The worst night of the week. Maybe it was the idea of having to go to school the next day after the weekend—although I always loved school. Maybe my parents put out a vibe about having to go to work. I don't know.

All I know is that it was the worst night of the week. And the loneliest.

In the evening, my parents and I would watch something together on TV, then one of them would read to me in bed as usual until I was sleepy. We'd go through our ritual of kisses and snuggles, then they'd turn off my lamp and leave my door ajar—they knew the exact distance it needed to be left open for me to feel safe. This was more or less the same routine every night of the week, but Sunday nights were the only ones when I'd be bereft when my parents walked out of my room.

Most nights, it wouldn't take me long to fall asleep. And if I couldn't, I was allowed to turn my lamp back on and read until I was ready.

But on Sunday nights, sleep would never come.

Something else would come.

It would seep through the floorboards, seep through the ceiling, seep through the walls. Soon, it would be everywhere in my room.

And then it would come for me.

Sometimes it stalked me and taunted me. I knew it was there and I'd breathe in shallow sips of air in the hopes that it couldn't see me, couldn't hear me. But as it came closer, I'd start to cry silent tears that melted down my cheeks and pooled in my collarbones.

Sometimes it was so fast that I wouldn't even get a chance to scream before it shrouded me.

I would gag on it,

choke on it,

suffocate on it.

And then my river would rescue me. The river that ran beside me, invisible to everyone but me. The river that rose and fell with my moods. My river would rise over me, always warm and soothing, enveloping me with its swells. I would try and sink down into it, desperate to escape the hopelessness.

"Take me away," I'd plead with my river. "Take me away."

Sometimes, I'd get out a scream and I'd hear hurried footsteps up the stairs or across the hallway, and one or both of my parents would be there, arms around me, kisses in my hair, words of comfort:

you're safe,

we're here,

it's only a nightmare.

The Sunday nights when it didn't come were almost as bad. The anticipation would eventually get me out of bed and see me tiptoeing downstairs. I would stand behind the wall leading into the lounge, and slowly peek around it. My parents would be on the three-seater sofa in front of the TV. My dad would be watching the Discovery channel; my mom would be reading a book, her feet across Dad's lap and her head resting on the arm of the sofa. Dad would be rubbing her feet, almost unconsciously. Apart but together. Solid.

I would stand and watch, willing one of them to turn their heads around and see me. And one of them always would.

"Oh, honey," they'd say. "Can't sleep?"

And my mom would sit up and cross her legs and I'd spiral into her lap. My dad would shift over and put his arm around her, and the three of us would watch TV until, too exhausted to fight it, I'd drift away.

My bad Sunday nights stopped once I started taking the meds when I was older. Or rather, the drugs diluted them and took the edge off, and I'd be able to talk myself down off the ledge.

But I still don't like Sunday nights.

I was thirteen when all the puzzle pieces fell into place. For months, I had been struggling to focus in class; I'd cry over anything; I couldn't eat and I couldn't get to sleep at night, and if I did sleep, I couldn't wake up; I didn't want to see any of my friends—I spent my weekends on my computer, playing games or surfing. I think my parents initially thought it was all just teenage hormones. They'd try and draw me out, try and talk to me, try to get me out of the house. After a while, they knew something was wrong.

And it all blew up on the day when I told my mom that I wanted to be dead.

We'd been drawing up our family trees in school. My teacher, walking around the class, commented on the age difference between myself and my siblings, and when she'd moved on, Susan Dyer turned around to me and said, "My mom says that you were an accident."

I didn't get it right away. She rolled her eyes.

"You know, a mistake. Your parents didn't actually want to have you. I mean, who has two kids, then waits, like, decades, before having another one. You," Susan said, "weren't meant to be born."

This was supposed to hurt me. But it didn't. All I could think about was her last words: that I wasn't meant to be born. It all made perfect sense now. I wasn't an after-thought. I wasn't even a thought. I knew that my brother was conceived before my parents were married, but I also knew that my parents wanted to have children—marriage wasn't what tied them together; it was their children.

But I was a mistake. An accident. I wasn't meant to be born. I wasn't meant to be. Somehow my soul had slipped through a crack in the lining between heaven and earth, and that was why I was fighting so hard to return home. Return to heaven. With joy, I told my mother this. I told her that I was meant to die.

# eleven

Sylvia drops me off at home after brunch. Earlier, I'd crossed my fingers and asked her if she was still going to the West Coast; she had replied that she was flying out the next day and would be gone for a month. This made me feel dark.

My mom comes out to say goodbye to Sylvia and exchanges a glance with her—I know Sylvia will be giving a report back over the phone later. As she drives off, my mom puts her arm around me.

"Have fun?"

I snap at her. "It was fine." I'm suddenly angry with her.

Leave me alone.

Breathe.

"Okay, so not so fine," I tried a laugh.

"What can I do? Did you have something good to eat?"

"I don't know. Yes, I guess, I ate fine."

I'm aware that I'm not making sense, but I'm so tired. I know that I need to do something, at the very least so that my mom won't worry. And I need to stop the anger from building up.

"I guess I'll go for a run."

"Okay, good call." She's relieved. "Throw on your sweats—I'll have some hot tea ready for you when you get back."

Exercise is another one of the weapons in my fight to feel good. Serotonin levels go sky-high when your heart-rate is elevated. But it's the absolute last thing that I want to do right now. I'd rather twist up in a ball on my bed

and scream

and scream

and scream.

And then sleep. But I've got to keep

moving,

moving,

moving.

So my sweats are on, my hair is tied up in a band, my earbuds are in, and I'm on the sidewalk.

They say that when endorphins are released during exercise, it's like being on a natural high. I've only smoked weed once. I don't smoke cigarettes, so I'm not entirely sure if I inhaled correctly, and I think I coughed most of it out before it got absorbed through my lungs, but I reckon I was on a bit of a high. I definitely laughed a lot. But it's got nothing on a runner's high. For me, it kicks in once I hit my second wind, and then I can run forever. When I walk, it's like I'm slogging through the air; when I run, I become fluid. And what's more, the high lasts for a couple of hours. It's not so intense as while I'm running, but everything is still easier afterwards.

On a good day, I can conquer the world after a run.

On a bad day, it keeps me going until bedtime.

On a *really* bad day...Well, I can't get up on a *really* bad day so I don't know what it would do.

My therapist suggested running as one of my strategies. Also yoga. I didn't really take to yoga. I attended a class for a couple of months with my mom. We bent, and stretched, and cracked, and groaned, and I'd leave frustrated that nothing had actually happened. My mom, on the other hand, loved it. I started making excuses as to why I couldn't go, and she went on without me. And still does. I'd never been much of a sportsperson—I played soccer for a while but wasn't much good at it—and running had zero appeal. But my mom found a training program and we started it together. Nowadays, I prefer running on my own. It gives me time to clear my head.

I walk first to uncurl my muscles. The pavement is cracked in places and I can't help but step over the zigzags. Walk on a crack, break your mom's back. Whatever that means. But with everything I put my mother through, the least I can do is prevent her from breaking her back.

The air is cold and sweet and I take in deep breaths to clear my head, and my heart. A breeze swirls and collects a handful of leaves left over from fall on the trees overhead and trickles them on to me. I shake them off, roll my shoulders and take off.

Fast.

I run until my heart is pounding in every part of my body.

I run until my legs ache.

I run until I can't cry anymore.

And then I stop.

I look around to get my bearings. I'm never quite sure where I'm going to end up. Once I had to call my mom collect from the pizza place right across the other side of our suburb—I had run too far to turn back. This time, I've run in a sort of U-shape; I'm only about four blocks from home. I cross the street, and it's then that I see the guy in the hoodie checking me out. His head tracks me as I walk down the road. Now, this is a pretty decent neighborhood, but you never can tell. I pull my buds from my ears. I'm really exhausted but I push my body into a kind of shuffle-jog to put more distance between myself and the guy in the hoodie.

Then I hear footsteps behind me.

I move the shuffle into a real jog, and try and remember something—anything—from that self-defense class my mom and I took two years ago. All that comes back is the bit about poking your attacker in the eyes and kneeing him in the groin. Like I needed a class to teach me that.

The footsteps are quicker now.

I can't go any faster so I take in my surroundings:

There's only a low wall between me and the nearest house, and I'm sure that if I scream, the occupants will hear me.

I spin around, arms in fight position, legs bracing, vocal chords at the ready.

I spin around, and come face to face with Sam.

Sam di Rossi and I used to be great friends when we were kids—two nut-brown children reflecting their past: mine when my great-grandfather took a beautiful Mexican bride; his from Italian grandparents. I inherited a love for the Spanish language, even though our ties with Mexico were severed the day my great-grandmother left with her American beau. Sam inherited his family's secret recipe for Arrabbiata sauce, which he could cook blind from when he was seven.

We were regularly mistaken for brother and sister. He would pull into my driveway on his bike and collect me, and off we would ride through the neighbourhood for hours; sometimes silent in our thoughts, but more often chattering and shrieking like gulls.

In the sunshine, he would show me how to light a blade of brown grass with his magnifying glass; in the rain, I would force him to take part in my elaborate plays.

He loved my house: Sitting around our kitchen table with milk and cookies, fighting over the remote control in the den, playing basketball in the driveway—my mom and Sam against my dad and me.

We were inseparable until he went on to middle school—he's a year older than me—and when it was pointed out to him by the new boy on the block that I was a girl. Gradually he stopped calling at my house, and like a tide going out, his visits receded.

He'll be back, I remember my mother saying.

We briefly intersected at middle school but by then we were worlds apart. Nowadays, I always see him around in the school halls: An imperfect reflection of the boy I used to know—so much familiar about him, but distorted by the ripples of time. He's much taller than me now but hasn't filled out his lanky frame. His hair is longer, lapping at his ears and the nape of his neck, and the sun has streaked it so it's a lighter brown than my hair. But his eyes, when they catch mine now, are still my twin.

They only catch mine for a second, because my aggressive stance clearly freaks him out, and he takes a step back, straight off the kerb. His legs come right out from under him, and the next thing he's on his butt in the gutter.

I can't help myself. I burst out laughing.

"Ow, jeez, damn!" he groans.

"Well, that'll serve you right for scaring the bejeezus out of me," I say.

"What?"

"Don't you know you shouldn't sneak up on people like that? Especially someone with a black belt in karate."

59

"You've got a black belt in karate?"

"No. But if I scare you, you'd probably have a heart attack if you snuck up on someone who actually does have a black belt."

Sam laughs.

"I wasn't sneaking up, though. You must have heard me."

"Sure, I heard a mugger coming up behind me."

He pulls himself up into a sitting position on the kerb, and he's checking out his hands—they took the brunt of his weight as he flung them out to save himself.

"Man, I'm sorry," he says. "I seriously wasn't trying to scare you. I wanted to check if it was you. I thought I saw you running past a couple of weeks ago."

The adrenaline pumping through me gives me the confidence to say, "That sounds a little stalker-ish."

He puts his hands up now. "Oh, no, no, not like that."

"So, like what? Doing a bit of neighborhood watching?"

"Oh, definitely not like that. Too 1984 for me."

"Do you mean the year 1984 or the book 1984?"

"Oh, I like the girl who knows there are two 1984s. And I mean the book. Big Brother and all that."

Did Sam di Rossi just say he likes me? He's not saying anything now, though.

Say something, Elle.

So I ask him, "What are you doing here, anyway?"

"Um, living."

"What?"

"Living. I live here, remember?"

I turn around, taking everything in now. He's right, this is his road. It's been so long since we've hung out together, that I've forgotten.

"Yeah," he says, "it's been a long time."

But not so long that he can't still read me.

I can feel a beat against my neck—for a second I think it's my pulse then I become aware that my iPod is still on. It's attached to the strap on my arm, so I reach for it to turn it off.

"What are you listening to?" Sam asks, getting to his feet.

"Um, I think that was Nirvana."

"Seriously? You're into Nirvana?"

"And you're so surprised, why?"

"No, I just took you for, I don't know, something different."

"Nirvana's not different enough for you?"

"No, I mean, I love Nirvana. I should have guessed since you hang out with that crazy Libby girl."

I raise my eyebrows.

"For whom I have much respect," Sam continues.

I lower my eyebrows.

"Just, how did you get into Nirvana?" he asks.

This is kind of embarrassing.

"Um, it was my dad."

"Your dad? How cool!"

Cool? Okay, then.

"Yeah, he'd been a bit of a rocker in his day," I said, "but I guess responsibilities got in his way until my older brother and sister hit their teens. That would have been, like, in the early nineties and grunge was in big time. My dad kept on hearing Sylvia and John's music and ended up becoming Kurt Cobain's number one fan, to their embarrassment."

"Embarrassment?"

"Sure, I mean, who wants their parents to enjoy their music—it's supposed to be something that you use against them; something to make you stand out from them. Johnny always said it's not so much fun when your dad's playing the same music even louder than you are. But they both got over it when he took them to see all the bands, like Pearl Jam, Soundgarden, Mudhoney, Screaming Trees and, of course, Nirvana."

"Ah, man," said Sam, dusting off his jeans. "Imagine seeing all those bands in their heyday."

"Heyday?"

"Did I say heyday? Ok, now that's *my* dad embarrassing me. He always says heyday. Guess it rubbed off on me."

"Yeah, it tends to do that. Like, my dad never quite got over Kurt Cobain's death so despite the fact that I wasn't even born in that era, there was always the sounds of grunge in the house and in the car when I was growing up. Couldn't help but love it."

Not surprising, then, that my tastes run to alternative rock and more recently, with the instalment of Libby in my life, hard-core neo-punk German bands. But I'm not going to tell Sam that. Or that I can't go for a day without listening to music. It's one of my strategies. It doesn't really matter what I listen to—any type of music lifts me. Even sad love songs. Maybe music takes my mind off my own emotions and for the three or four minutes that a song is playing, I'm concentrating on someone else's thoughts and feelings. I don't go anywhere without my iPod—it's my safety blanket.

Then Sam says, "I saw you at school yesterday. I wanted to talk to you."

I become aware that he is standing quite close to me now. Not too close to be uncomfortable, but close enough that the beat in my neck *is* my pulse this time.

"About what?" I ask, wondering what on earth Sam di Rossi wants to talk to me about.

"About...nothing. I don't know. Just talk. Like, how're you doing?"

Oh good, I think. I can answer that one.

I smile and look at him. He looks back.

"I'm doing fine," I say. "How are you doing?"

Suddenly the air between us is shimmering bright, like the sun skimming the surface of a lake. The air shakes as a car passes, and when it comes to rest, the shimmer is gone.

"I'm fine," Sam says softly.

I abruptly become aware that my face must be bloated from crying, and that I must be red and sweaty. I don't know why I care; it's only Sam. But I'm confused by what just happened.

"I gotta go," I say, my words stumbling. "My mom will be worried. I must go."

"Elle," he calls.

But I'm already halfway down the street, in a full-out sprint, my feet pounding out Sam's name until I'm home.

# twelve

There's a text message on my phone from Libby when I get back from my run: Hast Du unser Problem schon aufgelöst?

She definitely used Google Translate for that one. But I get the gist of it. The Problem is our lack of transport to the concert.

I phone my brother, Johnny, but only get his voicemail. I leave a message that I hope sounds a bit cryptic—he's useless at returning calls unless you entice him.

We're running out of options on how to get to the Besiegung concert and I need to have a plan in place before I tackle my mother. I spend the afternoon reading, and I'm still feeling good by the time I get ready for bed, even though Johnny hasn't called. I know the run gave me the happiness injection I needed but there's something else too. I take my meds, read for a bit, then select an easy-listening playlist on my iPod.

I'm tired, but a real muscle-aching tired. I fall asleep quickly, and I dream about Sam.

Sunday

# thirteen

Today is a *really* bad day.

Everything is drained of color. It's hard to explain—
I mean, if there is no color, surely I wouldn't be able to
see anything.

That would be cool.

That would probably mean that I am dead.

But I'm not. What I'm seeing is everything in one
color, but in different shades. I can't describe the
color—it's one that doesn't exist in our spectrum. All I
know is that it's awful—it's the color of pain and
hopelessness and despair.

Every day I open my eyes to the realization that I am
still alive. Sometimes I keep my eyes closed for as long
as possible and imagine what lies outside the darkness.
Heaven? Hell? Something in between? What will be
there when I open my eyes?

My mother's voice usually breaks through my
darkness, calling out from downstairs.

Then I open my eyes. If it's a good day, I get up.

If it's a bad day, I use my mantra.

Get up.

Get going.

Keep moving.

Keep moving.

Keep moving.

If it's a *really* bad day, then I don't get up at all.

I'm awake. My eyes are open. There's no color. I'm not moving. I'm not even sure if I'm breathing. There's water everywhere.

Then I hear my mom's voice. From her tone, it's obvious she's called out to me several times but I don't remember hearing her. She must be in my room now.

"Elle?"

I still don't move. I'm not facing her, but I am aware of the tension that draws her up into an exclamation point.

"Elle!"

I feel her shift across the room, leaving a gap in her wake, a gulp of air before the waves crash into the vacuum. My river is up to my neck now and I want to sink back and let it flow over me, but my mother has reached me and is holding me in her arms, holding me up above the water, and she isn't going to let me go.

"Let me go," I say inside my head.

"No," she says.

She's putting a tablet in my mouth and it melts down the back of my throat. She rocks me, swaying and singing. Time passes, and the waters recede, down to my shoulders, dripping from my arms, sliding off my legs. I fall asleep and when I wake up, hours and hours later, my river has receded. But it's still there, welling behind my eyes.

Monday

# fourteen

Today is a good day.

I can't explain why I've woken up to a good day. I don't know why yesterday was a *really* bad day and I couldn't begin to guess what kind of day I'll have tomorrow. I used to think there was a pattern but now I'm not so sure anymore.

But today? It's definitely a good day because I can see in color. You don't know how beautiful colors really are until you lose them. The book cover next to my bed is a swirl of blues and greens, the Besiegung band poster on my wall is made up of maroon and black and yellow lines, and the feather boa—from a long-gone fancy dress party—circles my mirror in a crown of purple. My eyes keep catching another pool of color and this makes me happy.

But do I still feel as if I should be dead?

Yes.

Only, maybe not today.

The problem is that if you say that you feel like you should be dead, most people immediately leap to the conclusion that what you actually mean is that you want to kill yourself. So if you say out loud that you think you should be dead, that's how you end up in therapy at the age of thirteen.

# fifteen

Libby didn't ever talk about our conversation in the bathroom of the football stadium. For a few months, I wondered if maybe she didn't remember what had happened. Until the day she asked if I wanted to a see a movie after school and I said that I couldn't because I had to go to therapy.

As I said it, I flinched. I'm normally really good at not mentioning this part of my life but I had let my guard down.

"Therapy?" Libby scoffed, turning several heads. We had a free period and were supposed to be studying. She glared at the faces looking at us, and we were left alone again. But my heart dropped.

"My parents made me go to therapy," she said, this time in a lower voice. "Didn't work out. Got fired."

"You fired your therapist?"

Libby snorted. "No. She fired me."

I must have looked confused because she said,

"Seriously. She fired me. Apparently, I was mean to her."

"How old were you?"

"About eleven."

"Jeez, how mean can…"

Oh. Wait. Forgot who we were talking about here.

"So how did you end up in therapy?" she asked.

I took a deep breath. I'd never told anyone this before.

"I sort of told my mom I wanted to be dead."

"Ah," said Libby. "I can see how that didn't go down well."

No, it didn't. It went something like this.

Me: Mom, mom!

Mom: What's it, honey?

Me: I've figured it out!

Mom: Figured what out?

Me: You, know. Why I'm not supposed to be here.

Mom (smiling): You've lost me. Not supposed to be where?

Me: Be here. Be alive. Susan Dyer said her mom told her that I was a mistake and that's why I'm not meant to be here.

Mom (not smiling): Oh, honey, that's not true! You know that…

Me (interrupting her): No, but mom, that explains everything! Like why

I'm not supposed to be here and why I want to be dead!

Mom (softly): What?

Me: I think I'm supposed to be dead.

And then she wrapped herself around me like a warm day, and I hugged her back excitedly. That's when I realized that she was crying.

"So," said Libby. "Your mom bundled you up in the strait jacket and took you straight to the looney bin.

"Something like that."

First stop on my road to therapy was, actually, to our family doctor. I had a full check-up along with blood tests—all part of what the doctor called a depression screening. I also had a session with the school counsellor—all about school and my friends and my activities. Her notes along with the comments from teachers were given to my doctor. I was anxious about what the teachers had said because I knew I hadn't been working well recently. School felt so hard. But my friends weren't finding it that difficult. For me, nothing seemed to sink in; I was present in class but I might as well have been in bed for all the good that it did me. I was also literally in bed a lot. I was falling behind and I couldn't see any way of catching up. Nothing positive was going to be in those teachers' reports and I was worried what my parents would say.

But they never said anything.

That was worrying too.

It turns out there was nothing wrong with me physically, but apparently I ticked all the depression boxes because the next thing I knew, I was in therapy.

Obviously it wasn't as simple as that. Or maybe it was. My mom sat me down and said, "Dr Haddon thinks that you should see a special kind of doctor. A therapist. That's the kind of doctor that you just talk to. We think it might help you figure out why you are so sad"—she gulped at this—"by talking to someone who specializes in helping people."

I nodded, thinking that maybe this person could help me explain to my parents why I'm not supposed to be here. Clearly my attempt hadn't worked.

Our doctor recommended a child therapist named Miriam Goldstein. Both my parents had a session without me, and it must have gone well because they returned home raving about her. Then it was my turn. I was nervous going on my own but Dr Goldstein had obviously convinced my parents it was the right thing to do because my mom practically danced me into the therapist's office, gave me a brief but firm hug and a "I'll be waiting right outside", before closing the door behind her and leaving me alone with the doctor.

I wasn't sure what to expect, but after pouring me a glass of water, Dr Goldstein introduced herself as Miriam, sat herself down opposite me, and we chatted. She was so easy to talk to, and she didn't ask any difficult questions or seem to be trying to trip me up. We simply chatted. And then it was over.

The following week we all saw her together.

"Depression," said Miriam from a lotus position on her sofa, "is a lifestyle choice."

"What?" protested my father, his adoration for Dr Goldstein quickly evaporating. "Are you trying to tell me that my daughter has chosen to be depressed? That suffering from depression is her choice?"

He was half out of his seat now.

Miriam smiled. She uncrossed her legs, put her feet firmly on the floor and rested her hands on her knees.

"That's not what I'm trying to tell you. What I am telling you is that Elle has some lifestyle choices to make. Elle," she said, focusing on me, "I need you to know that this is not a phase you are going through. Your parents understand this. Half the problem is trying to convince parents that what we're trying to deal with is not 'just a phase'. But your parents are on your side.

"However, if I am to help you," and she took us all in, "and I mean all of you, I need you to have a good understanding of what we're dealing with here."

She had our attention now.

"Depression is a dangerous condition. There is no quick-fix for depression. There is also no way to tell if this is the type of depression that eventually rights itself, or if this is something that Elle will live with for the rest of her life. It can even make itself scarce for years and then return when you're an adult. And that's what I mean when I say that it's a lifestyle choice."

She turned to me now.

"I'm going to say something harsh, Elle. This is your choice. You can live with depression. Or you can let it wilt you away until you die. I'm not going to sugar coat it. You can die from depression."

I had turned my head so I could see my parents. We had all latched onto the last sentence that Miriam had said—you can die. Both my parents were staring at Miriam, trying to digest what she had said. They had identical expressions on their faces: mouths slightly ajar and eyes blinking fast. They were scared. My parents' fears had been realized in that instant.

I could die.

But for me, it was something different. My fears had been allayed.

I could die.

I told Libby some of this. Not all of it. Not why I keep going to therapy when I don't think it really helps anymore. That why I keep going is to keep my parents happy.

# sixteen

~~

I don't mind the therapy. Which is just as well, as my mom has made me a lunchtime appointment for today. I usually see Miriam once a week on a Thursday but after this weekend's meltdown, an emergency session has been scheduled. I'm not at school today. Despite spending all of Sunday in bed, I've still managed to sleep in until ten this morning.

Miriam is in her early seventies, with hair showering down her shoulders in two falls of silver with her rimless glasses forming a strait between the two streams. She has the stereotypical shrink's sofa—leather, brown, long enough to stretch out on, comfy enough to rest your head on the armrest—but she says she claimed it as her own years ago when she found her particular style of therapy. On warm days, she sits cross-legged on the couch, her back as straight as an i, her head punctuating the top. In cooler weather, she curls up, s-shaped, under a silver shawl.

Her regulars—as she calls her patients—can choose between a bright blue beanbag, a sofa covered in a brown, patterned chintz, or her desk chair. I always sit in her desk chair. It's black and tall and can swivel around and around. Which is what I do during our sessions. Around and around until I'm dizzy. It would drive me mad, having to watch someone spin like that, but Miriam's never said anything, and I've been seeing her once a week for the past two years.

Our sessions have gotten into a routine. Miriam gets me a mug of cocoa—regardless of the weather—while she sips on herbal tea. Also being a tea person, I tried hers once. It smelt of freshly cut grass, and tasted like that too. Miriam laughed at my description.

I'd heard that therapy is a bit like talking to yourself and I didn't like the sound of that. I spend far too much time talking to myself. But Miriam makes therapy a conversation.

While sipping on our drinks, I usually relate my week to her:

a horrible assignment I had to do for homework;

how I twisted my ankle during dance class;

the argument I had with my mother over the health care system (health care should be free for everyone, I asserted; but who's going to pay for it then, my mom questioned; all the rich people, I answered);

the rude joke my brother told me during our weekly phone call;

how Libby and I saw a shooting star from my bedroom window on Saturday night.

Then Miriam lets me into her life:

the new juicer she bought that can squeeze the life out of a bunch of vegetables in 30 seconds (she offers to bring me a sample of her latest concoction, which she says *is* actually made from freshly cut grass);

how her windshield wipers keep switching themselves on and off for no reason, but refuse to work if it rains;

how her husband's doctor's appointment revealed he has only fifty percent hearing in both ears (and that's revealed the secret of our marriage, she laughed, he's only had to listen to half of what I say!);

and how she's really disappointed with the ending of a book she read.

But today's session is different. For some reason, even though it's not a bad day, I start behaving like a sulky teenager. I say no to a drink and I don't offer up any snippets of information into my life. I just rock on my chair.

Miriam doesn't beat about the bush, then.

"So," she says. "What happened yesterday?"

"Dunno," I say.

"Dunno," says Miriam. "Haven't heard that one before. Is that a friend of yours? Or an activity you had to do at school? Sounds Australian."

She knows she can get me to smile. And I do, weakly.

"But I really don't know," I say. "I went for a run the day before, I took my meds, I slept well. Then I woke up. And couldn't wake up."

"What about your diet? Did you eat anything out of the ordinary?"

"Mom did the food list. You know what's she's like—she's all over it. All over me. But there's nothing. There's nothing that I did or ate differently from the day before that or the day before that or the day before that."

I'm angry, and I'm crying. This is so unfair. I'm having a good day and now I'm crying.

"I can't," I say. "I just can't."

"You can, Elle. It was only one day."

"But it feels like every day! I know it's not every day, but that's what it feels like."

Miriam passes me a box of tissues. I blow my nose and it honks noisily. This makes me smile a little, and when I look up, Miriam's handing me a mug of cocoa. I roll my eyes at her, but I take it. Then she talks about her book club, whose members she despises but for some reason she can't get herself to leave.

I'm starting to feel better.

"Hey, you're supposed to be a therapist," I say. "Can't you figure out why you won't quit the club—aha, that's it! You always say that you never give up on your patients—maybe you can't give up on anything…"

Miriam laughs. "You've got a future career in therapy, that's for sure. But enough analyzing me—it's your turn."

I know where this is going.

"How's your river today?"

So… about my river.

When I was younger, probably about seven or eight, I became aware that I had a river. I could feel it running next to me, but if I tried to actually see it, it would disappear. I then worked out that if I concentrated on it, in my mind I could see it. It wasn't frightening or anything. It was just there. Its waters were a clear blue— I could often see right down to the pebbles on its floor. It made no sound, but I knew that if it did, it would be a light laugh, like a baby's gurgle. Sometimes, if I couldn't fall asleep at night, it would lap against me and it would soothe me to sleep. It wasn't hot or cold; there was no feeling of temperature when it ran next to me, but I could still feel it there. If I had to do something that was a little scary, such as stand up in the front of the class to do a book talk, my river would rise with me, and it comforted me.

I tried to tell my mom once about it when I was younger, but I couldn't explain it clearly and she didn't understand. I think she thought it was some sort of imaginary friend, or rather, an imaginary object, I suppose.

That's what it was like in the beginning. But as I got older, I noticed that my river started changing. If I couldn't sleep, it would still soothe me, but not by lapping against me. It would spread all around me,

rising and falling,

rising and falling,

but each time it rose, its tide would be a little higher. And the higher it got, the more I wanted it to shroud me entirely, to pull me down into its depths and take me away.

And I could physically feel it when it got like this. Warm on some days. Cool on others.

Sometimes it would do this in the mornings too, on the *really* bad days. It was the reason I wouldn't be able to get up because then it would enfold me in its waters and I would

sink,

sink,

sink,

and it would save me.

On my good days, my river would still be there, its sheer waters trickling gently around me.

On my bad days, it would be cloudy and fast-streaming.

On my *really* bad days, my river would be an angry sea; not angry with me, but with whatever force was doing this to me. And it would start to swell, rising and falling in time with my breathing, its tide coming in to take me away.

When Miriam asks me about my river, I do my usual song and dance.

"River? What river? I don't see any river around here."

I cross my legs, putting my elbow on my knee and stroking my chin with my hand.

"Do *you* see a river?" I ask her. "And how does that make you feel?"

Miriam smiles.

"It's still cute," she says. "But getting a little tired."

I twirl around in the chair so my back's to her.

"It's okay today," I say.

"Describe it to me."

"Um, it's quite clear. I can nearly see to the bottom."

"Do you think the new medicine is helping you?"

I swing around to face her.

"I guess."

"Any side effects?"

"I don't know. I think I'm more tired than usual, but that could also be because we're coming to the end of the semester."

"Lethargy is a side effect, though," Miriam tells me. "Will you try and monitor your tiredness over the next week?"

I nod. I don't know why I don't tell her that I'm having to take my anti-anxiety tabs nearly every day now. They're supposed to be for emergencies. They're going to run out soon and then I'll have to 'fess up. But for now, I want a little peace from all of this.

"I'm not changing your meds," says Miriam. "One really bad day is fine. Let's focus on the good days, because they've definitely extended over the past few weeks. What do you think?"

She's right. I have been having more good days. But it's hard to explain how one bad day can wipe out all of those.

# seventeen

~

"Okay," says Miriam. "Your mission, if you choose to accept it, is simple. You said your mom is 'all over you'. You often refer to your parents—particularly your mother—as controlling or smothering. I want to try and pin-point when you think this started happening—or if they've been this way all your life. I want you to close your eyes and think back to the first memory you have of your parents."

I close my eyes and spin around in her chair. I let time trickle through my hands. I see myself as I imagine I was as a baby; see my parents as I imagine them then, pieced together from old photos. I grow myself: now I'm two or three years old, maybe, walking between my parents and they're swinging me —one, two, three, swing!

I open my eyes.

"I don't know if this is a true memory, or if it's

something you see parents do with kids in the park or on TV and I've just made it into my memory. But I can see my parents each holding one of my hands and swinging me between them."

"And how does that make you feel?" asks Miriam, in a perfect parody of my earlier tone when I was trying to avoid talking about my river.

I smile at her.

"Touché."

Miriam cocks her head to one side, her hair a billowing wave of silver. She's still expecting an answer.

"It makes feel happy," I say.

"Anything else?"

"Safe, I guess. Knowing that they're not going to drop me. That between them I'm safe."

"Good work, Elle," she says. "So do you think that they still want to keep you safe? And that's why you feel smothered?"

"I guess. I mean, I know. They love me and don't want anything to happen to me."

Miriam nods.

"Now. Part two. I want you to think of the latest memory you have of your parents—a memory of them together."

Closed eyes. Spinning.

"Together," I say, my words whirlpooling with me.

"Yes, a memory of them together."

"No, I know. I mean, that's my memory. My mom saying 'together'. "

I heard my parents talking in their room one night recently. They always spoon in bed, with my mom's head tucked under my dad's chin, and his arm resting on her waist. In the mornings, I'd find them in that position, and when I was younger, I'd curl up into my mom's shape and she'd wrap her arms around me. And my dad would reach over and pat my head—I guess letting me know that he was there too—before returning his arm to my mom's waist.

At night, my mom would murmur about her day, often not even aware that my dad had drifted off to the soporific sounds of her voice.

But this particular night, as I moved past their door in the direction of the bathroom, I could hear my mother clearly.

"It's the impotence I hate," she was saying. "To feel that you can't help your own child is devastating."

I couldn't hear my dad's reply beyond the whisper that he breathed into her hair. Whatever it was, it made her cry. I felt like an interloper on their intimacy, but I couldn't get myself to move away. They couldn't see me—the door lent in just enough to shelter me—but I could hear the mattress sigh and I pictured my mom moving even closer to my dad.

"Together," I heard her say.

"She said, 'together', " I tell Miriam. "It made me so happy. I get why they call it a lump in your throat—I felt like I was swallowing a marshmallow."

"Why did that make you so happy?" Miriam asks.

"Because I knew that they'll always have each other. They'll always be together."

"They sound like they care deeply for each other. That they're still happy together. And that's important to you?"

"Yes," I say. "Because… Because they'll still have each other. When I'm gone."

"And where are you going to?"

I turn away.

"You know what I mean," I say.

"I want you to say it."

"But you know!"

She doesn't reply; she waits. I take a deep breath and say, "Fine. When I die. They will have each other when I die."

Miriam has tried to convince me to tell my parents about my river now that I have the vocabulary and understanding to explain it to them. But I can't. It's enough that they have to deal with me; taking on a river, I think, would be their tipping point. Don't get me wrong: my parents are the best. There is nothing they wouldn't do for me, and nothing they haven't done. It took me awhile to realize that my mom wasn't going in to work every day after dropping me off at school, and when I finally cottoned on, she explained that she was working mainly from home. I'm no genius, but even I worked out that the real reason was that she wanted to be near me. In case I needed something. In case I did something.

I've tried really hard—face-to-face and through Miriam—to convince my parents that I don't want to kill myself. But when you tell your parents at the age of thirteen that you want to be dead, I guess it's reasonable for them to jump to that conclusion.

And the incident earlier this year didn't help.

# eighteen

I'd been out for a run one morning about six months ago and when I returned home, I found my mom sitting at the kitchen table. I could see she had been crying, despite the make-up she had apparently applied to disguise the fact. Make-up can't cover the pain in your eyes. It scared me. Something was horribly wrong and my first thought was,

it's my dad,

he's dead.

Or Sylvia,

or Johnny.

"Elle," she said. "I..."

She choked on her words. Now I was terrified. Then she pointed at my laptop; I hadn't noticed she had set it up on the counter. I was confused, then I saw what was on the screen and I got it. I smiled at her in relief.

"Thank god," I said. "Is that all it is? I thought something had happened. Something bad."

And that's what triggered the avalanche.

My mom was up, out of her chair, and she was over me. All the words she had prepared—the kind, understanding, steadfast, supportive, enduring words I knew she would have prepared—were gone, and in their place was rage. And fear.

Let me explain: I'm a sucker for disaster stories. I know this makes me sound morbid, but it's not like some other disaster followers who feed off the misery of others or who get a thrill out of it. I lose a little part of myself every time I read or watch or hear about a plane crash, or a flood, or a tornado, or a tsunami, or a fire, or a collapsed building. But I can't turn away; my head is already so full of these thoughts, so one more isn't going to make a difference.

What I think about is how things would go down if it was me on that plane—

screaming,

crying,

praying,

dying

or in that building—

falling,

falling,

crushing,

dying,

or in that fire—

choking,

scalding,

burning,

dying.

So many different ways to die.

I've got news alerts for these types of stories on the internet and I get slightly preoccupied with them. Only Libby knows about my fetish, as she calls it, and she managed to work out, all on her own, why I did it.

"You're a sick puppy," she said at first.

But after scrolling through my browser history of horrors one day, she said, "I get it. You know you are going to die and these stories give you insight into a variety of ways of how you could die. But you're still a sick puppy."

She lifted her head from my computer. "So, if you could choose, how would you want to die?"

"By drowning," I answered immediately. Yeah, I'd given this some thought.

"Drowning?"

"Yes. I like the idea of being overwhelmed and swallowed up. I've read survivors' reports of drowning... Yes, Libby," I said, as I saw her about to butt in with a snarky remark, "Obviously they didn't completely drown; obviously they were resuscitated. But it doesn't mean that they didn't actually drown. Can I continue?"

Libby sighed—she doesn't like being caught out before she can be sarcastic—then nodded.

"So they say it's awful at first—that desperate fight against the water, searching for air and finding none, but refusing to give up. Until you do. Then it suddenly becomes peaceful; like your body and brain both register at the same time that it's over. And then you don't remember anything else until…"

This time Libby did get her say.

"… until you discover someone's French kissing you back to life?"

"Something like that."

"But you don't want to be French kissed back to life."

I didn't say anything. But, sure, exactly like that.

But this isn't what caused my mother to freak out—this is just the beginning.

I acknowledge that I've said I don't want to kill myself. But that doesn't mean I haven't been interested in the concept. In fact, that's why I know that I *don't* want to kill myself.

There are some websites out there for people planning their suicides. They discuss the various ways that you can do it—the pros and cons—and they support each other when the time comes for them to say goodbye.

The first time I came across such a website, I was horrified, then revolted; curious, then sad.

Then scared: What if I did want to kill myself?

I spent a lot of time dwelling on this, and a lot of time reading about depression and suicide. But I came to this conclusion: Even though I know that I want to be dead and that I know I'm going to die, this doesn't stop me from wanting to do things right now. I'm not trying to cram everything into my short life and I'm even making plans for the future. After I graduate, I want to spend a year in South Africa with my cousins and then go on to college. I'd love to have kids—I think I'd make a good mom. What makes me sad—on my bad days—is the thought that I'll never have any of this. But even on my *really* bad days, the ones when I *really* want to be dead, you couldn't make me do it. You couldn't make me kill myself.

It was a relief to find that out. But it doesn't stop me from sometimes going back to those sites. I find some comfort in them, thinking that maybe I don't have it all that bad if I'm not going to actually commit suicide.

It's also made me think about committing suicide. What I mean is not the action, but rather the words. It's a peculiar combination of words: to commit suicide. One of the sites actually discusses this phrase. It says that the word suicide comes from Latin: *sui*, of oneself, and *cidium*, a killing. The killing of oneself. Why do we then link it up with commit, meaning to do something deliberately? The word suicide implies that it's deliberate. I guess you can accidentally kill yourself. But I've never heard anyone say, "It was accidental suicide." And people don't say, "He suicided" in the same way they say, "He murdered". You can commit murder. You can commit a crime. Suicide was actually seen as a crime years ago, so I can see how these can be linked. With all the time I spent and still spend scrutinizing these sites, I've got a better understanding of why some people do it. So surely a kinder way of phrasing this act of despair can be found?

He died from suicide.

He died by suicide.

It was this searching for some answers that caused the incident. I'd been doing some reading on the internet the night before, surfing suicide websites and reading stories about people planning their own deaths, or about the people who have been left behind and how they are dealing with the death of a loved one.

The next morning I went for a run. I never asked my mother afterwards why she was using my laptop. It certainly wasn't something she did often—or possibly ever—or else this would have happened a long time ago. But it didn't matter to me. What mattered was that my mom had opened my laptop, and my browser was still running, and the page on the screen was a blog run by a woman who was discussing exit bags.

If you didn't know what an exit bag is, then you'd be perplexed as to why my mom had hit the roof. If you knew that an exit bag is a bag with a drawstring that you slip over your head—after taking an overdose of tablets as well as anti-nausea meds to stop you from throwing up—that you then tighten around your neck before you pass out so that you end up inhaling your own carbon dioxide, then you might comprehend her reaction.

This might make it clearer: Another name for an exit bag is a suicide bag.

So my mom went hysterical and I couldn't really hear what she was saying. She was crying and yelling, then sobbing and whispering. Then she put her arms around me and held me so tightly that I felt as if she was squeezing all the air out of my lungs.

"Stop," I told her. "Mom. Stop. I'm not going to kill myself.

Please.

Listen.

Stop.

I'm not, I'm not."

I was stroking her hair, trying to calm her down. I was cursing myself for being so stupid. Stupid for leaving that website open and stupid for not understanding sooner why she was so upset.

I tried again.

"Mom. It's not what you think. I promise. That's not me. I won't. I promise."

"Then why," she said, so very quietly, "are you reading about exit bags?"

"Look," I said, manoeuvring her onto a chair, then reaching for the laptop. "I need you to read this."

"I've read it." I could only just hear her, and she wouldn't look at me.

"No, really read it. Read it as if you don't have a daughter who you think wants to kill herself."

She shuddered, but she turned her head up. I placed the laptop in front of her and sat down next to her.

"This isn't a site about *how* to commit suicide. It's about people who *want* to commit suicide. I know, I know, it's hard to see the difference, but what I've been reading about is *why* these people want to kill themselves. And they're not me. I don't identify with them. I'm not them. I don't want to."

I could see she was trying to focus on the words

through her tears. I showed her another site—a group of people who, yes, were planning to kill themselves, but weren't talking about that. They were talking about why. It's clear they've found kindred spirits in one another, but this isn't enough to stop them. They just want to talk. And then at some point, they'll kill themselves.

"But mom," I said. "I'm not like that. I don't have a 'why'. And that's why I'll never do it."

It's weird thinking about this now; some of those people on those sites are probably dead.

# nineteen

~

Miriam and I end our session today no closer to figuring out what caused my *really* bad day, but one thing I do know is how lucky I am. I give my mom a hug when she collects me; I can see this makes her pleased. Then I groan when I see the pile of papers on the back seat of her car. She's been to school.

I might miss quite a lot of classes, but I don't miss out on anything. My mom has a copy of my schedule, and she rounds up from my teachers whatever I need to catch up on. So that's my afternoon finished. But the groan was more for effect; I know she's doing the right thing for me, and my self-confidence is way better now that I can sort of keep up with my classes.

"Oh," says my mom on the drive home, "Johnny phoned me. Said you'd tried to get him over the weekend. Something about the road less travelled? He had no idea what you're on about, but he said to call him after your session."

Thank god I'd been cryptic in my message to Johnny. I'm feeling good about my parents right now, but not that good that I'm ready to tell them about the festival. I ring Johnny from my room when I get home.

"Bad timing, Elle," he says, after I explain what I need. "I'm taking Hope away for the weekend."

Hope is his latest in a series of girlfriends. He follows such a predictable pattern:

boy meets girl,

boy dates girl,

boy invites girl home to meet parents,

boy takes girl away for weekend,

girl starts planning future,

boy dumps girl.

"Oh, no," I say. "I really like Hope. Please don't break up with her."

"What? I didn't say that. I said we're going away for the weekend."

"Johnny."

"Argh, not you too! I don't have a pattern!"

"Listen, Friday isn't technically the weekend. When exactly are you leaving?"

"On Friday."

"Friday night?"

"Friday day."

"And you can't leave a bit later?"

"Not if we don't want to arrive at Breaker's End at midnight…"

"And is this weekend away set in stone?"

I'm trying to stay upbeat but my heart is falling fast.

"Afraid so," says Johnny. "But ask Mom to take you."

"They've got Simon's memorial service."

"Ah. Well, there must be someone else going."

Then he stops. He realizes who he's talking about.

"Or maybe...."

"Yeah, or maybe…"

"What does mom say?"

I'm quiet.

"You haven't told her," Johnny says.

"Nope," I say. "What's the point? She's not going to let me go with anyone else."

"Sorry, Elle," he says. "If it was any other time. I feel like I'm letting you down."

"You are. You've chosen taking Hope away so you can break up with her over going with me to an amazing concert."

"Hey, that's mean!"

"I'm kidding, I'm kidding, you know I'm kidding. Sort of."

"Do you want me to talk to mom?"

"Maybe. But I'll see if I can come up with another plan first. Don't worry about it."

But this is all bravado. I get off the phone feeling pretty devastated. Johnny was my last resort. There isn't another plan.

# twenty

I'm not great when I get into bed. I broke the news to Libby earlier, who didn't take it very well and called Johnny all sorts of creative names in German. I spent the afternoon plodding through my schoolwork so now I'm tired. But I know I'm going to struggle to fall asleep. My meds are taken and my music is on, and my river is around me when I lie down. It's lukewarm and it's skimming over me.

Something like this shouldn't bother me that much. Missing a concert is not the end of the world. But right now it feels like it is. I'm breathing deeply, swallowing the air to stop me from crying. But it doesn't work. My river is rising and I am sinking.

_Tuesday_

# twenty-one

Today is a good day. Who would have guessed? And, as it turns out, a *really* good day. I haven't had one of those for a while.

I open my eyes this morning and I'm still alive. But I don't feel as bleak as I usually do when I discover that I'm still alive.

I get up without any difficulty, and before my mom comes to wake me up. I meet her coming up the stairs and she smiles at me and I love the expression on her face when she realizes I'm having a good day.

When I arrive at school, the sun is shimmying across the plastic facade, giving it an almost organic, alive feel, and I take the stairs two at a time.

I get through the first half of the day without incident. It's the second half when things go weird.

# twenty-two

The first thing happens during Spanish. Libby, Savannah, Julie and I are all in the same class, and before the teacher arrives, Libby's got us huddled around Julie's desk.

"Right," Libby says, "first on the agenda for today..."

Savannah groans. "Really, Libby? An agenda?"

"...is the Besiegung concert."

"There is no way in hell my mother will let me go," says Julie. "Zero chance. Zip. Nil. Null, as Besiegung would say."

"So let me get this straight," Libby says to Julie. "You're not coming?"

Julie throws her a dirty look.

"Right then," says Libby. "Go back to your desk."

"I'm at my desk," says Julie, narrowing her eyes.

"Libby," I say.

"Well, what use is she to us now?"

Julie scrunches up a piece of paper and lobs it at

Libby, but misses, and then turns to me.

"My mother won't let me watch R-rated movies," she says. "Not a chance she'd let me go to a concert."

She cocks her head.

"Think you might be in the same boat as me," she says.

"Don't I know it," I say.

"Have you spoken to your mom yet?" Savannah asks me.

"God, no. I need the perfect opportunity to speak to her about it. I've narrowed it down to either when she's asleep or when she's nowhere near me."

"What's the big deal?" asks Savannah. "Your mom will probably drive you all the way there, read a book in the car while she waits for you, and then drive you back. Like she did that time we had that birthday party on Demi's ranch."

I stare at my hands and clench them into fists.

"That's the big deal, Sav," I say. "I don't want her to drive me. I want to go to the concert without my mother attached to my hip. And besides, my parents aren't going to be here."

"Oh," says Savannah. "So even if you manage to convince her to let you go, how exactly are you going to get there?"

I grin at her.

"You cow!" Savannah says. "That's the only reason you want me to go with you guys!"

I have the decency to look slightly ashamed, but Libby's having none of it.

"Dude, you've had your driver's license for over a month—isn't it time we go on a road trip?"

"Does the fact that I don't even like that awful band bother you at all?"

"There are, like, 10 other bands playing," counters Libby. "I'm sure you'll find at least one that can carry a tune to your satisfaction."

"There's just one problem with your brilliant plan," says Savannah, flicking her hair back. "I'm not around this weekend."

"Right, whatever," says Libby.

"No, I'm serious. We're flying out on Friday morning to spend the Christmas break at my grandmother's. You know this. I told you guys."

"What the hell?" snarls Libby at me. "Now what the freak are we gonna do?"

I'm not feeling quite the pain that Libby is. I knew that Savannah was never going to be able to take us anyway. She only ever drives to school and back—I don't think she's driven on a highway before. And I knew trying to convince my parents to let me go with her would be a nightmare. I'm still hoping, I don't know, for something, though.

Libby's on to the next thing.

"You know what you could do," she says to me.

I know. I know exactly what she's talking about. I could tell my parents nothing. I could go to Libby's, then we could find some way of getting to the concert, then go back to Libby's, and my parents would be none the wiser. Of course, at some point they might phone

Libby's mom and then all hell would break loose. Anyway, I'm not going to do that. I'm not that kind of girl. After everything that I've put my parents through, I can't add lying and deceitfulness to the list. I know that by telling them, this could mean that I don't get to go to the concert. But I can't imagine a scenario where not telling them and having a good time at the festival would coincide.

"Two reasons why I can't do that, Libby," I say. "One, I don't want to. Two, I don't want to."

Libby stage sighs. "How is it that I'm friends with such a goody two shoes?"

"Oh," says Julie. "I've just remembered."

"What?" Libby and I both ask at the same time.

"Oh, nothing to do with the concert. It's only that Sam di Rossi was asking about you in the car park this morning, Elle. Wanted to know if you were in school today. Care to explain?"

When she realizes we are off the topic, Libby turns to wheel herself to her desk, but then she pauses, her back to us, waiting, I guess, to hear what I have to say. I'm blindsided.

Why would Sam be looking for me? And why are the next words out my mouth a lie?

"It's nothing. I've got something of his."

Mr Herrera walks in and I shrug and skulk to my desk.

# twenty-three

Libby and I always meet for lunch in the cafeteria. It's a grim place. The sterile-grey benches and tables are supposed to create an appearance of cleanliness but it misses its mark by about the whole target and comes off looking like a prison dining hall. And the bits of food ingrained in the scratches on every surface only confirm what both of us already know—that the cafeteria is a breeding hell-hole for every kind of evil bacteria we can think of. Neither of us ever buys anything here. Libby refuses on the grounds that cockroaches and rat droppings do not form part of her diet, while my mother still packs me a brown paper bag daily.

My mom, being my particular mother, has done extensive research into what foods can be considered— as she calls them—happy foods. The latest fad is berries. She read a snippet somewhere that berries can improve your mood, so berries it is. Our fridge is always filled with them—black, blue, red, straw; if it's got berry in its name, we've got it. I think my mother feels helpless if she can't actually do something; it's not enough to just be supportive and loving and understanding—she needs to be physically doing something to help.

She's also got me on a strict diet. Not so much a diet as a healthy eating plan: Eating three meals a day at almost the exact same time each day with two small meals tucked in between these, as well as provision for a before-bed snack. A dietitian who specializes in drawing up eating plans for depression sufferers was consulted, so I follow a high-protein-with-only-the-good-type-of-carbs diet. Really, it means that I need to eat healthily and regularly, which I was doing pretty much anyway, but again, it makes my mom think that she's doing something.

I've also got my drug store at home. Apart from my antidepressants and anti-anxiety medication, I've also got a shop-load of vitamins—Vitamin A through E, selenium, beta-carotene, omega-3, and a couple of others whose names I can't really pronounce.

To be honest, I'm not sure if any of this helps. On my bad days, it doesn't matter what I eat. Those days stay bad. And I've tried to monitor what I eat to see if there are any triggers, but it seems pretty much arbitrary. I like being healthy, though, so I eat whatever my mom puts in front of me.

And at least it makes one of us happy.

Libby's supposed to make her own lunch but never does, so I've got to ensure mine stretches to feed two mouths. I'm sitting at our usual table—nobody dares steal our spot for fear of Libby's wrath—and I'm munching on my cashew nuts, watching the cafeteria fill up with kids in jeans and hoodies, girls in daisy dukes and tank tops despite the weather, boys in sagging pants and band t-shirts, Goths in black, jocks in blue, hippies in the colors of a rainbow, and feeling the vibe in the room change from hospital morgue to coffee shop hangout. This is when the second thing happens. Someone swings onto the bench opposite me and says, "Hey, didn't I used to know you?"

It's Sam.

# twenty-four

"Seriously?" I ask. "That's all you have to say for yourself? That's the best you can come up with?"

Sam's face darkens and glows. He's bending towards me, with a flop of hair over one eye; now he pulls up straight.

"What?" he stammers.

I give a slow grin that I know starts in my eyes. He relaxes.

"Jeez, Elle," he says, "you really had me going there."

We're both grinning at each other.

"Hey, dude, get out of my seat."

Libby has arrived. Sam leaps up.

"God, sorry—here, sit."

"Sam," I say, "she's kidding," tilting my head at her wheelchair.

"As you can see," says Libby, "I come with my own built-in seat."

He glows again.

Libby rolls to her customary spot at the head of the table, and leans in to see what's in my lunch bag. Sam's still standing. I raise my eyebrows at him, and he sits back down.

"Libby," I say, "you know Sam."

"Of course I know pretty-boy, star-of-the-football-team, honors-roll Sam."

"Um," says Sam. "I think you're confusing me with someone else—I don't play football and I'm not on the honors roll."

"Ha," says Libby, "but you don't deny being a pretty boy."

I flinch.

Sam doesn't. He's got his groove back.

"When you got it, Libs, you got it. Far be it from me to deny it."

I flinch again.

"Dude," says Libby. "Did you call me Libs? Stronger and certainly better-looking men have suffered and are still suffering for that."

Sam grins.

"My apologies. I know what it's like to hate having your name changed."

"Oh, so you're a Samuel, are you?"

"Nope, plain old Sam. I just hate being called dude."

They glare at each other, but Libby has had more practice at this.

"Dude," she says to him, "pass me my lunch bag."

He doesn't move. Then he grins again and hands it

over. Libby peers into it, and takes out one of my sandwiches.

"So," says Libby to me. "Did you give him his thing back?"

I don't get it right away.

"You know," she says. "That thing of his you said you have."

I can feel the heat in my face and right now I could kill her. But Sam must be thinking about something else because he says to me, "So, Elle Marshall. Tell me what you've been doing over the past—how long has it been? About six years?—over the past six years. I want to hear all about it."

At that moment I wish I have Libby's attitude. I wish I know what the right thing is to say. Especially the exact right thing that would make him stay sitting here with me. Because my heart is pounding, my ears are singing and my palms are actually sweating.

"Where to start?" I say. "A lot happens to a girl over six years."

Damn. I didn't mean it to sound like that. I didn't have breasts the last time Sam and I hung out together. But he saves me.

"Remember the time we tried to build that treehouse in your backyard, and I somehow managed to get a rope wound around my neck and I fell and you had to hold me up so that I wouldn't throttle myself while you yelled for your mom?"

"Clearly," I say. "And you didn't 'somehow' manage to get the rope around your neck; you actually tied it around your neck—you said it was a good place to store it while you climbed the tree."

"No," Sam says, "that's not how I remember it. But moving along…"

The table shudders as Libby makes her presence known by bashing her footrest into the leg.

"Really," she says. "Are you guys going to 'remember when' for the whole of lunch? In that case, I'm outa here. You," she says, pointing at me, "I will speak to later."

And with that, she's wheeling out. With my sandwich on her lap, of course.

"Whew," says Sam. "That's one scary chick."

"Oh god," I say, "don't ever let her hear you call her a chick. That one you will not survive."

We both grin at each other, but in an instant the air between us starts to shimmer, so I break from his gaze. I shift on the bench and my foot touches something under the table. Please don't let it be his foot, I pray. Sam doesn't move.

"But seriously," he says. 'I'm sorry we lost touch.'

"Well," I say, "I didn't really stand a chance after Michael Saunders moved up the road."

"Who's Michael Saunders?"

"Oh, nice," I say. "You don't even remember who you rejected me for!"

"No, wait," he says. "He was the kid with braces? I think he moved to California a couple of years ago."

The bell rings. Something moves under the table. Oh god, it was his foot.

"Elle, this was real," Sam says. "Any chance we can do it again sometime?"

"You know where to find me," I say, inwardly rolling my eyes. Really, Elle, that's the wittiest thing you can come up with?

"Same time, same place tomorrow then?"

I stand up and give him what I hope is a mysterious smile but which I'm pretty certain makes me appear constipated.

"How can I be sure?" I say. "Last time I said goodbye to you, we didn't speak for six years."

"Because," he grins, giving me a once over, "as you said, a lot can happen to a girl in six years."

Dear heaven. I can't do anything else but walk away.

# twenty-five

I'm coming down from the track after practise when I hear someone call my name and I turn. It's Sam again. He's coming towards me with a couple of other guys, but he bounds in front of them and suddenly he's right beside me.

"And," he announces, "you thought you'd have to wait another six years to get to talk to me again."

I give him a look, and carrying on walking.

"I meant to ask you at lunch," Sam says, seemingly undeterred. "What happened to you yesterday? I heard you weren't at school."

I try and play it cool.

"Oh, now he misses me?" I say.

"You're never going to let that go, are you?"

I shrug in what I hope is a nonchalant way.

"So, were you sick yesterday?" he asks.

"Yeah, a migraine."

This is my standard response, invented by my

mother to protect me.

"A migraine?"

He pauses.

"Didn't you used to get them as a child too?"

I nod, surprised that he remembers.

The pause is longer this time.

"And do you still see that river?"

My steps don't falter, but my heart does. In my mind, I can see my whole body being jerked backwards in slow motion. But my steps do not falter.

"What river?" My voice is only just above a whisper, and I clear my throat.

"Oh, never mind," he laughs. "I've been thinking a lot lately about when we used to hang out together, and I've got a stupid memory about some river. Forget it."

I regroup quickly.

"Forgetting," I say. "Something you do well."

"Jeez, Elle."

"Hell hath no fury…"

"Will it help if I apologize?"

"Maybe."

"I am sorry—truly, deeply sorry—for forgetting about you."

"Nope," I shrug.

"What?"

"Hasn't helped."

"I give up!"

He turns to go, but then whips back.

"Just kidding."

He swings behind me and in a swift move, lopes my

schoolbag off my shoulder and onto his.

"I'm going to make it up to you one chivalrous act at a time."

I raise my eyebrows questioningly.

"Can I give you a lift home?" he asks.

I don't respond. I can't. His eyes have twinned with mine and I can't move. And it seems like he's having the same problem. We're in a vacuum. I don't know how long we stand there, staring at each other, until a voice breaks the bubble.

"Dudes, get a room."

Air rushes around us, and Sam staggers back.

"Elle, your mom's here," says Libby, her voice controlled and cold.

I become conscious of the fact that we're standing in the car park.

"My mom fetches me," I say stupidly to Sam, and I take my bag from him.

Now I'm on autopilot—my mom has opened the back door and I scoop Libby into my arms and put her on the seat. My mom folds up the wheelchair as I open the trunk and we tuck it away together. My mother hovers for a second. "Everything okay?"

I nod. I can breathe properly again. Everything is okay.

My mom straightens up and I hear her say, "Hi Sam", as if it hasn't been years since they last spoke.

"Hi, Mrs M," says Sam naturally, and I take a peek at him. His hands are tucked in his jean pockets, and he looks, well, he looks like Sam. He doesn't look as if something just sucked all the air out of the universe and then blasted it back in again. What he does do is look right back at me.

Then I'm in the car and my mom is driving away.

"Well, well, well," she says, without taking her eyes off the road. "So Sam is back."

# twenty-six

Libby doesn't say a word on the way home and neither do I. We let my mom fill the silence. We hear about her day: Her first (failed) attempt at online shopping; her second (failed) attempt at writing a paper she's supposed to be delivering at an upcoming conference; her accidental turning on of the TV and compulsive watching for two hours of some reality show.

Then we're at Libby's, and we're getting her into her chair.

"Bye Mrs M," she sings to my mom. Libby's never called my mother anything but Mrs Marshall before. I don't even get a wave.

"Trouble in paradise?" asks my mom, as we drive off.

"You know Libby," I say. "Never know what's going to come out of that mouth of hers."

We share a smile.

"So you're having a good day, then," my mom says.

"I guess those meds must be working."

She pats my knee as we pull into our driveway.

"Well, something's working anyway," and she makes wide eyes at me.

I leave my phone on silent when I'm at school, so it's only when I get to my room and dump my bag on my bed, that I see the light flashing on my phone that's peeking out of my jeans' pocket. Eight calls from Libby; no messages. I sit cross-legged on the bed, brace myself, and click on her name.

"What the hell?"

"And a hello to you too," I answer.

"What was the deal we made, dude? What was the damn deal?"

I hesitate. Should I plead ignorance? Not worth it.

"I know what the deal is."

"Say it, Elle. Say it."

"No boyfriends."

The irony of this, of course, is that Libby has had dozens of boyfriends. Despite the bad attitude and perpetually bad hair days, boys can't keep away from her. And she went through a phase of not turning them away. I understand why now; she'd deny it to her grave, but she was trying to find someone to like her for her. Not for the girl in the wheelchair. Not for the hot chick. And not for the independent hot chick in the wheelchair. Just for her. So she tried out nearly everyone—she dated a guy from the swim squad, and one from the chess club; one from the school newspaper, and one from the glee club. And once a boy who was known to bat for the other side. She tried them all. And not to mention—in words you might find familiar—the pretty-boy, star-of-the-football-team, honors-roll Ricky Mansfield, the hottest and most popular boy at school. None of them lasted more than a month and she was always the one that did the dumping.

I, on the other hand, have had exactly one boyfriend. Simon Taylor. Or Simple Simon, as Libby calls him. To his face. But that was one of the reasons that I liked him; he was simple. There were no complications, no deep, troubled discussions, no arguments or fights. Of course, this meant that the relationship didn't last very long. But he was the first boy who kissed me good and proper. I did kiss another boy after that. Okay, two other boys. But no boyfriends. It was difficult enough to get through some days; having a boyfriend attached to those days made it nearly impossible.

So when Libby and I became friends, we made a pact. She would give up serial dating, and I would stick with kissing the odd boy in the hall. But no boyfriends.

"That's right, dude. No boyfriends."

"Libby. I don't have a boyfriend."

"Not yet, you don't. But you two might as well have pledged your undying love for each other right there in the parking lot this afternoon. And don't"—as I start to interrupt her—"try to deny that something happened today."

I don't say anything. I don't have anything to say.

"Hello? Don't tell me I've offended you. I've said

worse things before."

"I'm still here, you idiot."

"That's more like it, dude."

"Libby?" I ask. "What the hell was that this afternoon?"

"God alone knows, dude. All I know is that when I rolled up, you two were making out with your eyes."

I giggle.

"Ah, dude, what's with the freaking giggling? Come on, you know that's my kryptonite."

I get up and close my bedroom door, sliding down the inside of it until I'm on the floor.

"Libby," I whisper.

"What?" she stage whispers back.

"He knows about my river."

"What the? You told him!"

"No, dude, no!"

There was a pause from both of us. Libby breaks the silence.

"Did you call me dude?" Her voice is incredulous. Almost awestruck.

I never call anybody dude. Not even dudes.

"Sheesh," I say. "I've been spending far too much time with you."

"Woohoo!" shrieks Libby. "My powers are great!"

Then she's back to business. "Now what the freak do you mean that he knows about your river?"

I had told Libby about my river quite a while ago. I'm not sure if she got it—she kept saying after that that she wanted one of her own—but I'm never sure with Libby.

"I must have told him when we were kids. It's not like he knows what it is; he only remembers something vague about it."

"Okay, but that doesn't explain the eye-kissing."

"The what? No, don't answer that."

We are both silent again. It's my turn to break it.

"Libby, he does something to me. Something, I don't know, magical. And shut up."

I can hear her moaning under her breath. "Magical. Jeezus freak, she said magical."

"This conversation is over," I said.

"You're telling me. You're lucky the friendship's not over too. Freaking magical."

And she hangs up.

# twenty-seven

I haven't even put my phone down when it rings. I answer: "I thought I said that this conversation was over—unless of course you'd like to start a new one…"

Libby doesn't say anything. But Sam does. I recognize his voice right away, even though I haven't spoken to him on the phone in years.

He says, "Um, I'd like to start a new one, please?"

"Sam?"

"I guess you were expecting someone else…"

"No, yes, I mean, Libby and I… oh, don't worry."

"Elle?"

"Um, yes?"

"Hi."

I close my eyes tight, and then open them.

"Hi, Sam."

I'm under control now but I'm thinking, how did he get my number?

"I guess you're wondering how I got your number,"

he says.

"Well, no, but now that you mention it…"

"Ok, so you know my friend Jacob, or maybe you don't, but anyway Jacob's in a band with Noah Taylor's brother—you might know Noah? He plays basketball? But anyway, he's dating Alexis, who's in your social studies class. So Jacob asked Noah's brother—I forget his name—to ask Noah to ask Alexis if she had your number. And turns out you two did the diorama project together so she did have your number. Although the diorama was for the drama club. So I guess you're also in the drama club with Alexis."

I could hear him run out of breath and then suck in some air. I decide not to help him out so I don't say anything.

"Uh, hello?" he says.

"Hmm," I say. "That is an interesting story. Thanks for sharing."

"I guess that does make me sound a little stalker-ish. Again," he says.

"You think?" I say.

He starts again, but I interrupt him.

"Sam," I say.

"Yip," he says.

"Hi," I say.

"Hi," he says.

Then neither of us says anything. For a while. Like for a whole minute. But it's not odd; I like that he's there, on the other end of the line—not a line, anymore, is he on the other end of the air?—and I feel as if I've sunk down into my mattress, my head on the pillow, my eyes closed, when actually I'm still sitting on the floor and my eyes are wide open.

Then Sam says, "So," but he draws it out. "Soooooooo. Now I guess you're wondering why I'm phoning."

"That did cross my mind," I say, lying through my teeth. I wasn't questioning why he was phoning; the voice in my head was chanting,

Sam's on the phone,

Sam's on the phone,

Sam's on the phone!

I don't care why. Just that he is.

"Well," he says. "I really enjoyed catching up with you today. I don't know, I keep seeing you all the time—out running, and in the hallway, at lunch, in the parking lot—and I think maybe fate's trying to tell us something."

"Fate," I say. I feel all weak, but manage to get out: "And what exactly is fate trying to tell us?"

"That, maybe, we should be friends again."

"Friends," I say, calmly, while the voice in my head yells,

Friends?

Friends?

I don't want to be your friend! I want us to be I don't know what I want us to be but I know that I don't want us to be friends!

"So, how about it?" asks Sam. "Friends?"

Be cool, Elle, be cool, says the voice.

"Woah, buddy boy," I say. "Not so fast. I've got enough friends. Why would I want to be friends with you?"

"What? I am offering you a once-in-a-lifetime opportunity to be friends with—how can I put this?—a pretty-boy, star-of-the-football-team, honors-roll dude—and you're questioning this?"

"Listen," I say, "I think we established today that you're no star-of-the-football-team, honors-roll dude."

Huh, imagine that, I said "dude" twice in one day. Twice in one hour. I must tell Libby.

"And," I said, interrupting what I know will be some comment on his pretty-boy status, "you ain't no pretty boy."

"Ah, stab to the heart," he cries, and then goes all serious. "But I have other qualities too. I make a mean Sloppy Joe. And I'm very funny. So funny in fact that I even make myself laugh. I'll be sitting all by myself and suddenly a really hilarious thought pops into my head and I'm off! Rolling on the floor with laughter. Now that's not a quality you find very often in someone. I mean, lots of people are funny but they're only good at making others laugh and not themselves."

"But," I say, "the important thing is this: Do people laugh at you, or with you?"

"Does it matter? Either way, I get myself and other people laughing."

"So you're a clown. That's one of your qualities."

"I like to think of myself as a street performer, rather than a clown, thank you very much."

I'm running out of witty things to say. Well, not that I've been witty, as such, but I think I've been able to hold my own. Now I have no idea what to say next.

Fortunately, Sam does.

"Listen," he tells me. "I know you're probably a bit overwhelmed at this point so I'll give you some time to think about it."

Before I can respond, he says: "So, have you thought about it?"

And again, he butts in: "Just kidding! Boy, that Sam and his sense of humor… And now I'll take my leave, potential friend, and bid you good day."

And the phone goes dead. But not for long. It beeps. I open the text.

"So," it reads, "have you thought about it?"

Okay, so he does make me laugh. At least, chuckle a little. But I don't know why I'm so conflicted. It's only Sam. But something bizarre keeps happening whenever I see him. Something—don't hate me, Libby!—magical. And now after talking to him on the phone, I want to get up and tear over to his house and… and I don't know what, but I need to see him right now.

Right now.

My mom breaks through my mind ramblings.

"Elle," she calls out. She must be downstairs.

I reply, but my voice is gruff, so I clear my throat and try again.

"In my room!"

I hear her footsteps on the stairs, and I get up and open the door.

"I know you're in your room," my mom says through gritted teeth, although she doesn't seem cross. "I was calling you to come downstairs."

"So why didn't you say that?"

"Because I didn't want to yell," she tells me. "Because you have a guest."

"A what? Who?"

"Sam."

My blood whirlpools.

She winks at me. "Anything I ought to know?"

"No," I say, then with more force than I intended. "No!"

"Sorry I asked," she says, taking a step backwards and holding her hands up in surrender. "Well, are you coming downstairs? I'm not sending him up here."

I shove my phone into my pocket and follow her down, on autopilot.

Sam's standing by the front door, his thumbs hooked into his back pockets, and he's looking up at me standing on the bottom step. I hear my mom say, "I'll make something to drink," but I don't really register that she's left the room because Sam is still looking at me and I'm looking at him and I can't look away and I don't think he can either and I can hear him breathing, rapidly, but it's my breath too, so we're both standing there, panting, and I need him to come over here, I need him to be right here, and then he's moving towards me and I'm leaning towards him from the bottom step and he reaches up and his fingers are coiling in my hair and my phone rings.

# twenty-eight

I finish my tea at the kitchen table in almost one swallow but my mouth is still dry. Sam's staring into his coffee mug as if there's some sort of clue in there that would explain what happened. My mom's pottering around but then says, "Just heading to the study to do some work," and she's gone.

"I'm sorry," Sam says immediately, not looking up.

"For what?"

"For what happened in there."

He tilts his head towards the hallway.

"What did happen in there?" I ask.

"I guess it's more like what didn't happen."

"So what didn't happen?"

"I didn't kiss you."

I swallow so hard that it hurts my throat.

"So you're sorry that you didn't kiss me?"

I'm not trying to flirt with him but before I can think

of what to say next, he stumbles, still talking into his mug.

"No, no, that's not what I mean, I mean I'm sorry that I didn't kiss you too but what I mean is I'm sorry that I did that in your hallway, but I don't know what happened and I wanted to and I can't look at you because something weird happens when I do and so I'm not going to."

His eyelashes are long and are covering his eyes and I want to reach across the table and stroke them with the tips of my fingers. But I don't. I just say, "I know what you mean. It happens to me too. The weird thing."

"Really?"

I'm starting to get more in control. My phone ringing when it did ended the spell in the hallway, and shocked us into backing away from each other. My phone rang and rang and we both glanced around as if we didn't know where we were and we didn't know where to look but all we knew was that we couldn't look at each other. At least, that's how I felt. Then my phone went silent, which was almost as startling, and my mom called from the kitchen.

Now my breathing has returned to normal and my heart doesn't feel as if I've been running.

"Sam," I say. "I think it's safe now. I think you can look at me."

"Really? Are you sure?" Some warmth has crept back into his voice and it's firmer. "Because I can't be responsible for anything that happens if I do."

"I'm willing to risk it."

Okay, so now I *am* flirting with him. He slowly raises his head, leaving his eyes for last, and then we're both looking at each other. And everything is fine. We grin at the same time.

"Hi," Sam says.

"Hi," I say.

"Sooooo," he says, "you're probably wondering what I'm doing here."

"Actually, what I'm wondering is how you got here so quickly. I mean, one minute we're on the phone and the next..."

"It was supposed to be a joke."

"Ah. A street performer joke."

"Exactly!"

"Forgive me for being stupid, but what exactly was the joke?"

"Well, thanks to the wonders of technology, I was actually phoning you from across the street. After I said that I'd give you some time to think about being my friend, I was supposed to ring your doorbell and say, well, have you thought about it? And then you'd laugh hysterically and you'd know exactly how funny I am and then I would offer to make you a Sloppy Joe to seal the deal. But things went horribly wrong. I saw you coming down the stairs and it all went weird and I tried to kiss you, which is not a very friendly, friend-like thing to do. So I guess the joke backfired."

When my mom said Sam was here, when I so desperately wanted to see him, I thought for a moment that my wanting him had summoned him here. Before I can stop myself, I'm saying, "I thought I had wished you here."

"Wished me here?"

"Ha ha," I say.

What?

What am I doing?

Sam's tilting his head to one side and I guess I'm supposed to be explaining myself, but all I can come up with is...nothing. I take a slow sip of my tea, hoping to buy myself some time but too late I realize my mug is empty and I end up making a loud slurping sound. A tide of heat comes over my face.

"Cute," says Sam.

I put my mug down.

"You're cute when you blush," he tells me.

Oh god.

Before I can say anything—although what am I going to say to that?—Sam speaks.

"I thought it would be better to see you in person. Thought I might be more convincing. I mean, that's why I came here."

"I thought it was a joke."

"Yes, but not a joke like I'm joking; a joke like it's meant to be funny and make you laugh, and I want to make you laugh because, well, you seemed sad today."

This startles me. Because I am sad so often, I thought I'd become quite good at beaming an aura of seriousness around me, rather than sadness. This is a worry, because today is a good day, so I can only imagine what I must appear like on a bad day. I'm not sure what to say.

"Sorry," says Sam. "I don't know why I said that."

"It's fine," I say, realizing how I can cover up. "It's only, Libby and I are desperate to go out to a festival at Fort Nottingham this weekend, but technically she's grounded, and my parents will be away, and we're starting to run out of options."

"I'll take you," he says, all at once.

I smile. "That's okay. It's like 300 miles away and we only want to see one band, and the band is, well, shall we say, not to everyone's taste, so it would be a waste of time for you, and, but, I mean, thank you for offering."

Sam shrugs and there's an uncomfortable moment. But then he looks at me, really, really looks at me, and although there's no shimmering air this time, just his deep brown eyes, I still can't turn away from him, and he says, "I really want to take you."

I can feel my chest moving from my breath. He's still watching me, and now he starts to smile. He leans in, not taking his eyes off me, and he says, "I love road trips. I love festivals. I love bands—all kinds of bands. I love those little mini-donuts they sell at those awful farm stalls along Route 17. Oh, you know what else I love? Picking an unmarked road to drive along to see where it goes to. I haven't road tripped in ages, and I've only once road-tripped without my dad tagging along...And I've never road-tripped with you before."

I bite my bottom lip.

"So what do you think?"

What do I think? Sam di Rossi has tried to kiss me,

told me that I'm cute when I blush, and offered to drive me halfway across the state to watch a band he's probably never heard of. If I died right now, I'd die happy.

Wait.

I don't mean that. That's an expression. My thoughts on being dead are not that flippant. I don't want to die now. Moments like this, then I don't want to die at all. But I can't ever shake the idea that I'm still not meant to be here. Even now. Even when my heart has become fluid and filled my whole chest and I'm smiling, even though I don't want Sam to see me smiling because I'm supposed to be playing it cool like Sam di Rossi offering—wanting—to go on a road trip with me is nothing out of the ordinary. Even now. Even on a good day.

There is of course only one small problem with Sam's suggestion. But I'm not going to think about that now and I deflect the issue on to something Sam would possibly understand.

"Libby," I say.

"No, of course Libby can come too. I didn't mean only us. Just us would be fine but I know Libby would have to come too. She does, doesn't she?"

This last part, I think, isn't said very enthusiastically, and I don't blame him. Who would want to spend a whole day in a car with Libby, unable to escape?

But I say firmly, "She most certainly does," in defense of my friend, and also knowing there wouldn't be any other way.

"So call her."

"Now?"

"No time like the present."

I really don't want to have a conversation with Libby on this subject in front of Sam, but my brain is in no position to come up with a plausible explanation, what with every ounce of blood in my body now located in my chest cavity, so I phone her.

Straight to voicemail.

Relief.

Her phone is off or she's on another call. Either way, I think as I hang up, I'm off the hook... I nearly drop the phone as it rings in my hand.

I know that it's Libby before I even see the name on the phone—I have the same ringtone for all my calls, but somehow when Libby phones it sounds sharper, angrier. And I'm right. I hold the screen up to Sam. He squints at it and then recoils in mock terror.

"Answer it, answer it, before she hexes us all!"

I wrinkle my nose at him but I answer.

"So what's with this ignoring me?" says Libby. It was Libby's call that had interrupted Sam and me on the stairs. "You know you're supposed to be at my beck and call. And don't roll your eyes at me."

I stop mid eye-roll and pretend to be examining something on the ceiling when I remember Libby can't actually see me. I still haven't even said hello, or anything for that matter, but Libby's in full swing.

"So plan F," says Libby. "I invoke my poor little crippled girl status and find a sponsor to chauffeur us to the concert. Isn't there like a Make-A-Wish Foundation for cripples? Or is it only poor little dying kids who get that?"

"Libby, jeez, you are so going to be struck down by lightning. That is uncool."

"Cool, schmool, who cares. All I care about is how the hell we're going to get to the freaking concert."

"Well," I say. "I might have a plan G."

Sam meets my eye then we both look away.

"Okay, enough of the suspense. Plan G?"

"You might not like it, though."

"Does it involve you and me getting to the concert?"

"Well, yeah, obviously."

"Then I don't give a damn. Spit it out."

"Sam."

"What does pretty boy have to do with it? Hope you're not still going all googly eyes over him."

I cover the whole phone with my hand in panic. Did Sam hear that? I sneak a peek across at him but he's tracing figures of eight on the table with his finger. I get up and walk to the window.

"Sam has a car. And a license. And, most importantly, a willingness to take us to the concert."

"I'll bet," snorts Libby. "But what does he want in return?"

"Nothing. I mean, I don't know. We were talking about it and he offered and so now I'm putting it on the table."

"You were talking about it? When?"

"Now."

"Now? On the phone?"

"Well, no. He's here."

"Did our conversation from, oh what, a little under an hour ago, mean nothing to you at all?"

"Jeez, Libby, could you be more dramatic?"

"How about, one more word about that dude and this friendship is officially over. How's that for dramatic?"

"Libby," I hiss, moving even further away from Sam. "What does it matter if it means that we get to go to the concert?"

There's silence. She's still there, though; I can feel her seething through the ether. But I know her. She's trying to decide whether to invoke the no-boyfriend clause of our friendship, or to take the ride to the concert. Potential ride. Possible ride. Oh god, what am I thinking? There is no way my parents will let me go with Sam. Libby knows this too.

"Your parents will never let you go."

I sigh. "Listen, let me deal with that. We're not there yet. All I want to know is yes or no to Sam being plan F, G, H—whatever plan we've got up to."

"Fine. Whatever."

And she's gone. I grin at the dead phone and then turn back to Sam.

"She's in."

Sam rolls his eyes. So Libby doesn't have that effect only on me.

"Like drawing blood from a stone, apparently."

I sit back down at the table, then I'm suddenly aware

that I've sat down right next to Sam. I push back on my chair in a bit of a panic.

"I'm not going to bite," he says, clearly amused.

But I've gathered my wits.

"I was more worried about you trying to kiss me again."

Of course, as soon as I say this, I realize I've nixed any chance of that happening again. Although right now, out of the moment, I'm not sure if I want it to happen again. Not like this.

"Ouch," he says, and draws back.

I squirm for a moment, and I think he's a little uncomfortable too, but then he says, "Okay, so we've got Libby onto Team Roadtrip. Now what about your parents?"

"Yes," I say. "About my parents."

"I'm going to take a flyer that they're not going to be too happy about you coming with me."

I start to interrupt, to object.

"No," he says. "I know it's not me. It's not personal. It's anybody. No parents in their right minds would let their teenage daughter go off with a guy they barely know."

He's staring at the table now.

"Didn't this used to be a different colour?"

This year it's olive green. Back in his day, it could have been anything.

"Yeah," I say. "Interesting observation."

"It's just I remember sitting at this table. Your mom made those awesome chocolate brownies. Good times."

They were good times. I suppose having Sam as a friend back then was like having a sibling. A brother. Oh god, I hope that's not what he's thinking. Because I'm certainly not thinking of him like a brother now. I'm not sure what he's thinking when he says, "What if I get my dad to invite your parents around for supper tomorrow night, and then they can grill him on what a superb driver I am and how awesomely responsible I am—I am both of these, by the way, and I'm pretty sure I can convince my dad of them too, ha, ha—and they'll be so blown away that they'll even let you marry me."

He stopped short, his eyes wide.

"Not that we're thinking about getting married. Or anything. Nothing. Just a saying. Just that they will definitely let me drive you—you and Libby, and whoever—whatever. Arrgh, Elle Marshall, you make me feel like I'm still ten when I talk to you! I feel so stupid!"

I don't know what to say. I'm still trying to get my brain from dinner at his house with my parents to getting married. So I laugh.

"Cute," I say. "You're cute when you get stupid."

He runs both hands through his hair in a way that it makes me want to as well. Run my hands through his hair, I mean, not my hands through my own hair. God, he makes me stupid too.

"So what do you think about my plan? Good? Bad?"

Um," I say. "Thing is, I kinda haven't even told my parents about the festival yet."

"Oh," he says.

"It's complicated. So I'm waiting for the right time."

"I get it," he says. "It's cool. But you know that today is Tuesday? And the concert's this Friday?"

"Yes. I am very aware."

"Okay then. So."

"So?"

"So when are you gonna tell them? You have to do it tonight."

"Jeez, Sam, you sound like Libby. So no pressure."

"It's just that you've got me all excited. For the concert, I mean. I was planning on getting a laser tag session in with Mike and Jonah, and now I could be road tripping to a music festival."

"Sam, you do know that the concept of a road trip isn't exactly meant to be over only one day? We'll be there and back in like ten hours. And we'd have to go straight there—no exploring little side roads."

"Hey, it's a trip. And there'll be a road involved. Voila—road trip."

He pauses for a second, then carries on. "Did you notice that you spoke about it in the future perfect tense."

"In the what?"

"Sorry, a bit of geek coming out in me. You said, 'We'll be there and back.' We will be there and back. We will. As in we will be going."

"Oh Sam, a mountain to climb first."

"But we'll do it together. You get them to at least consider the idea, and I'll slam dunk it home with my charm."

He makes me smile, despite the unease around my heart.

"You'd better get working on that charm, my friend," I say. "I haven't been party to any of it yet."

He clutches at his chest. "I'm so confused. On the one hand, I'm hurt that you have been immune to my charms. But on the other, my work here is done."

He stands up and slaps the table.

"You called me your friend."

# twenty-nine

As it turns out, I don't ask my parents today.

I'm cutting it fine, I know, but Sam doesn't understand—doesn't know—what the end of a day is like for me, no matter how good it's been. But I figure if I ask them in the morning, there'll still be enough time to arrange a meeting with Sam's dad for in the evening. It'll work.

No.

It won't work.

They won't go for it.

It's pointless.

I'm going to quit while I'm ahead. This whole thing is going to open a door that I'm not sure I'll be able to close, and is it really worth it over a concert?

Even if it is Besiegung?

There's a part of me, however, that knows this is not only about being able to go to a concert. It's about my parents letting me go. Just letting me go.

Even though I remain on a high from my *really*, *really* good day, I still pop my meds and put on my music. I've learnt my lesson in the past. It doesn't matter how good the day is, this is no indication of what the night will bring.

Wednesday

# thirty

Today is a good day.

And despite my misgivings, it had been a good night and a good sleep.

But it's not a great day. My river is churning a little, as if it's getting ready for something. Or expecting something. But it's still good, and I can live with that.

I'm awake before my parents, so I pad downstairs to put on coffee for them. I'm barefoot and my feet are cool on the wooden floor; I take in the uneven spots and occasional cracks and I wriggle my toes against the grain while I wait for my tea to draw. On my bad days, I'm surrounded by a fog that dilutes all my senses; on a good day, sometimes it's as if I'm feeling for the first time.

I take out three mugs—my dad's is the one that reads, "World's Greatest Dad!", my mom's is covered in roughly painted flowers of all colours, and mine is the next one I can find in the cupboard. I'm not picky when it comes to mugs, but my dad insists on his, even though there's a chip on the edge, and my mom appears faintly disappointed if I bring her anything but her flowered mug.

I hear them on the stairs and I pour the coffee.

# thirty-one

My dad's making pancakes and my mom and I are sitting at the table, finishing our hot drinks, and I'm feeling good, and I know this is it.

"Guys, I'd like to talk to you about something."

My mom, in the middle of a sip of coffee, raises her eyebrows, and my dad makes a "hmmm" sound.

"So there's this music festival on Friday. This Friday. In Fort Nottingham. And Besiegung is playing."

"Besiegung?" says my dad. "Seriously? They're coming here?"

"I know, I know!" I say, suddenly hopeful at my dad's enthusiasm. "It's unbelievable! And...and I'd really like to go."

"This Friday?" My mom is ahead of us as usual. "It's Simon's memorial service. We won't be here. You'll be at Libby's."

She turns to my dad, who's putting the pancakes on the table. But he's still with the band.

"You said they're due to release another album soon—I wonder if they'll showcase anything new?"

"I don't know," I say. "But how cool would that be?"

"When you say this Friday," says my mom, "do you mean the festival is over the whole weekend, or just on Friday? Because we will be back by Friday evening and could take you on Saturday..."

"It starts on Thursday afternoon and finishes on Sunday. But Besiegung's only playing on Friday. Only on Friday," I tell her, the last part spoken quietly.

"Oh," she says. "So. Well, I guess Libby's mom can take you. Um, I'll need to talk to her first; it's quite a distance and I'm not sure it's a good idea..."

"Libby's mom can't take us. Won't take us. She's angry with Libby again. She said we can go but that we'll need to find our own way."

My dad's up to speed now. He glances at my mom, and then sits down beside her, protectively.

"Elle, I'm not sure. We're not sure. How would you get there?"

"I've even tried Johnny, and he's not around this weekend. But I really want to go. Dad, you know how much this means to me."

I can see my mom is thinking, trying to come up with a solution.

It's now or never.

"And Sam di Rossi's offered to take us. He's nearly 18, he's been driving for ages, and he says we must all go and have dinner at his place tonight so you can chat to his dad about it, and none of us will drink or do anything stupid, we'll go there, watch Besiegung, they're playing first in the morning, only one set, very short, and then we'll come straight back, nothing stupid, we'll watch and come back..."

I fade a little at the end. My mom's shaking her head almost imperceptibly, and my dad's pouring honey over the pancakes but his mouth is set.

"Oh, Elle," says my mom, and she doesn't say anything else; well, not with her voice, but her face is saying, "Don't do this to us, Elle, don't do this."

"Please, Mom. Please. It's not fair. I don't ask for much. I do whatever you tell me. I know that I've hurt you"—she starts at this—"but I'm good now, I'm better, and I'm sixteen—you can't keep me wrapped in cottonwool forever, and I know you're scared, but I'm not going to do anything, and Libby knows everything and she knows I'm not going to do anything, and you know what she's like, she won't let anything happen to us, and Sam's a good guy, and he's a good driver, and..."

My dad breaks in.

"Honey, we know, we know. Listen, go and get ready for school, and let your mom and me chat about this— I'm sure we can make a plan."

My mom's expression at this is one of "Wha-at?", but my dad's hand is on her arm and gives it a rub. I don't want to look at my mom anymore; I know all of this is my fault—the fact that everything I do has to be scrutinized and I'm the reason why she's sitting there terrified—so I turn and leave.

It's just me and my dad in the car and we're nearly at school before either of us speaks. And then we both start at the same time, which actually makes us smile.

"I'm the oldest so I get to go first," says my dad. "What I'd like to ask is that you give your mom and me a bit more time to get our heads around this. You're an amazing girl and we love you so much and we trust you and of course you should be able to go to see your favorite band but..."

"There's always a but," I interrupt.

"But," my father continues, "but we'd like to think this through and make sure that we're making the right decision. It's hard for your mom—hard for both of us—to see you growing up so fast, and I promise you that there are lots of parents who'd also be thinking twice about letting their teenage daughter drive hundreds of miles with a teenage boy to see a rock concert..."

"But I'm no ordinary teenager," I say. "Let's talk about the elephant in the room."

We've pulled up into the parking lot, and my dad says, "Can we talk about this later? When you get home? I promise you everything's going to be okay. We knew this day would come..."

"Jeez, dad, you'd think I'd asked you if you'd let me

go and live in Thailand in a commune with drug dealers, or something!"

"Your mother and I are well aware that we are not necessarily reacting in the right way, in a fair way," he says, almost sadly. "But you have to hand it to us that we've always tried to do our best. Please give us some time."

I'm worried I'm going to cry. I feel like I'm breaking his heart. So I skim a kiss across his cheek and scramble out the car and I don't look back.

As I walk up to the school buildings, I give myself a talking to. Seriously, I'm getting so worked up over this damn concert that it's affecting my mood. And that's not good. It's just a band. That I'm madly in love with, of course. But still, just a band. And if I don't get to go, it doesn't mean anything. And it doesn't mean that I won't get to see Sam again.

What?

No, that's not where these thoughts were supposed to go.

I'm saved from any more of these thoughts by Savannah and Julie, who're waiting for me on the steps.

"Well?" says Savannah. "How did it go?"

For a moment, I'm not sure what she's talking about. How did it go with Sam?

"Your parents. The concert. Hello?"

"Oh, yeah, um, well, not sure yet. But it's out there."

"You mean you actually asked them?" This is from Julie.

"Yip. I take it you haven't asked yours."

"Nope. And you know what, I'm not going to. I think I'm going to bide my time for something I actually want to do more than life itself, rather than something that Libby wants us to do."

"Way to stand up for yourself, Julie," says Savannah, meanly.

"Oh please," she says. "If you weren't going away, you'd so be driving Libby to the concert, with or without your parents' permission."

"Quit it, you guys," I say. "Let's focus on me."

They both grin. It's not like me to want the spotlight on myself and they both know it. Julie's nickname for me was wallflower for ages before I finally got her to stop using it.

"So," says Julie. "What did they say? Your parents? When you asked?"

"Well, naturally from their reaction you'd have thought I'd asked them to let me fly to the moon. Not so much my dad, but my mom freaked. In her own quiet way. She didn't even drop me off today; my dad did. I didn't get an answer out of them directly—they're going to discuss it; probably are discussing it right now."

"Ouch," Savannah says.

"But you know what? It's not the end of the world if they don't let me go."

"Oh yes it is," says Julie. "Libby will make it the end of your world."

I swear that Libby hides around corners and listens in to conversations in order to make a dramatic entrance because here she is now with, "Who's world am I ending this time?"

Julie shrinks into the wall—hah, who's the wallflower now?—but Libby's not interested in her.

"So."

"So," I say. "It's out there."

"And?"

"And that's all. For now, anyway."

"So they didn't say no, is what you're saying."

"But, Libby, they didn't say yes."

"Not saying no is good enough for me. That's a yes in my world. Onwards. Where's Sam? I gotta see this car he's allegedly taking us in."

Savannah is onto this.

"Sam? Di Rossi? What's he got to do with this?"

Libby has a gleam in her eye.

"Nothing much. Only that he's taking us to the concert."

"What?" both girls squeal.

"Since when?" says Julie, her voice rising.

"Since he's crushing on our friend over here." Libby nods at me and now I understand the gleam in her eye—I spot Sam getting out of his car in the lot below us and I'm blushing.

I grab Libby's handles and start pushing her chair but I realize she's got the brakes on and she's not letting them go.

"What's the hurry, dude?"

"Libby. Please please please."

The chair surges forward and we're up the ramp into school but not before I hear the twin voices of Savannah and Julie. "Hi, Sam." And then giggles. I scrunch up my eyes and now I'm practically running to the safety of our home room.

# thirty-two

I don't see Sam at lunch—not that I was looking—and it's only before my last class that I turn the corner in the hallway and Sam's right there, his back to me, talking to a girl by the lockers. Blood streams up to my face and I can feel my heart pumping it there. It hurts. How did I get here? A week ago, I hardly noticed Sam. Okay, I've always noticed Sam, but only on the periphery of my world. How did he manage to now be in the center of it? I don't want this. I don't want to be this way. I spin around and walk away and then his breath is on my neck and his voice is in my ear and my name is on his lips. I don't turn around. I can't. Then he swings around me, asking, "You okay?"

"No," I say.

What?

I meant to say yes.

Why am I telling him I'm not okay?

"What's wrong?" I've hung my head and I can see

he's standing at an awkward angle, trying to see my face.

"Nothing."

"So you're not okay but nothing's wrong."

My heart's slowing down now, and I realize I'm acting stupidly. I'm trying to figure out whether just to keep my mouth shut, or maybe run.

Fast.

Away.

But Sam stops me in my tracks.

"They said no, didn't they?"

I let out my breath.

"Not exactly."

"How not exactly?"

"Okay, so they didn't say yes, but they didn't say no, and they're going to talk about it, and we'll talk about it after school."

"Promising?"

"I don't know. I don't think so."

"Hmm, delaying tactics. Typical parents."

I laugh humorlessly. Definitely not typical parents.

"So should I confirm supper with my dad? I've already spoken to him, and he's cool."

"Sam, I don't know. I don't think so."

I'm aware that I'm repeating myself, but I'm not sure in which direction to go with this.

"Listen," says Sam, "they're going to say yes. No doubt. And you can ring me this afternoon when you know for sure—my dad's good with impromptu stuff."

He touches my elbow lightly with his hand.

"Come on. You're going to be late for whatever

you've got now. I'll walk you."

Someone bumps against my bag and I become aware that other kids are walking around us but for that moment, I really felt as if we had been alone.

Sam doesn't say anything else as we walk, then I see that we're near my next class.

"Thanks," I say.

"Anytime," he says. "Although, thanks for what?"

"Thanks for doing all this."

"Hey, I haven't done anything yet. It's all up to you now..."

He's wagging his finger at me and walking backwards away from me, and collides with a guy coming in the opposite direction.

I use the confusion to duck into the classroom; any longer in his presence and I will...

I don't know what I will.

But something.

# thirty-three

Libby's with me when my mom pulls up in the school parking lot at four on the dot. Then my mom's out the car and she's smiling and opening the trunk and chatting to Libby and then we're all in the car and we're driving and she's still chatting to Libby and I realize that she hasn't actually spoken to me. And hasn't made eye contact.

I've threatened Libby with all sorts of torture if she even mentions the concert in front of my mom, but still she says, "So, Mrs M, what do you think of Sam?"

I don't move, but inside I'm clawing out Libby's eyes with my fingernails.

"Sam?" says my mom. "Oh, I like Sam. Always have. Did you know that he and Elle used to be best friends when they were little?"

"No," says Libby, punching the back of my chair. "I did not know that. Besties, you say? That explains it."

"Explains what?" says my mom, as I reach behind

my seat and attempt to slap Libby.

"Their connection. They've got this—oh, how to put it?—this magical connection."

Finally, my mom glances at me, and then turns back to the road.

"Libby," I say, aware of a tremble in my voice.

"Yes, Elle," she says, innocently.

"Can we please talk about something else? Oh, I know, like how you've got detention for the whole of the first week of school next year. Tell my mom what you did."

"Oh, Libby," says my mom. "What did you do?"

There's very much a "this time" implied at the end of her sentence.

Libby's not ashamed of her numerous escapades that land her in detention, so I know she's eager to tell the story.

"Well, you know Mr Hardcastle? He's our English teacher? I figured out that he's got something going on with our home room teacher, Ms Taylor, but I can never catch them at it. So we had to make up a poem—lame, I know—about romance, and I wrote this awesome one about unrequited love, which ended in,

"Like Esmeralda and Quasimodo

Like Juliet and Romeo

Like Maureen and Leo"

"Okay, I know the first two couples," says my mom, "but who are Maureen and Leo?"

"Ms Taylor and Mr Hardcastle," Libby sniggers.

"Oh, Libby."

"So then I volunteered to read mine out to the class, and when I came to the end, Mr Hardcastle went bright red and I thought he might have a heart attack."

"Okay, so that's a bit off-center, but surely not worth detention?"

"I guess I took it too far. As I went back to my desk, I asked him how Mrs Hardcastle is."

"There's a Mrs Hardcastle?"

"Yip!"

"Oh, Libby."

Since I was actually there for the scene that Libby had created, I'm not really listening. What I am doing is trying to figure out how this is going to go down when I get home. Mom seems bright and cheerful. Too bright, though. Like she's pretending. When we get to Libby's house, I help Libby into her chair and push her to her front door, not something I usually do. Then I punch her on the arm, hard this time, and she winces.

My voice is low when I say, "What the hell? How could you bring up Sam?"

"Testing the waters with your mom. You heard her, she likes him."

"Yeah, when he was eleven! And Sam's so not the issue here. You know that."

I give her chair a last push and I storm back to the car. I take a deep breath before I get in, and then pretend to fiddle with my shoelace for the rest of the way home. As we pull into our driveway, my mom asks, "Can we talk?"

I don't want to do this in the car, so I start getting

out and say, "Sure. Shall I make some tea?"

"That would be nice."

We're both being super polite. I don't like this at all.

We're standing in the kitchen when she starts.

"Your dad and I chatted this morning."

"Hmm," I say, pretending to be very focused on finding the tea bags.

"I'm not... We're not happy about this festival. I'm sorry that we can't be here to help you. I rang Libby's mom this morning, and she's not budging. She's really mad with Libby. I'm not sure I understand her logic that Libby can still go, despite being grounded. And I tried, Elle. I really tried to persuade her to take you guys, but she's adamant that Libby needs to learn her lesson."

I'm pouring hot water over the teabags, and I'm trying to keep my hand steady.

"Mom," I say. "I know all this already. This is not about Libby's mom taking us. It's about Sam taking us."

"Well, Libby's mom's not thrilled either about Sam. I don't mean Sam. She doesn't even know Sam, which is the point, I guess. So it's not just me."

I can't believe it. She's trying to turn this into an ordinary dilemma of should the teenage girls be allowed to go with the teenage boy. Which it's not about. It's all about my parents not wanting me to do anything. Anything that doesn't involve them, of course.

I snap at my mom, "You're so fake."

She's stirring her tea now, and the spoon clunks against the cup.

"Elle, that's not nice. And what does that actually

171

mean, anyway?"

"It means that you're trying to convince me that no sane mother would let us go with some boy to the concert. Libby hasn't even spoken to her mom about Sam yet. Give her five minutes with her mom, and she'll be in the car with Sam and off to the festival. And you know that. So what happens to your little argument after that?"

I know that I'm being rude. My mom and I rarely fight, and when we do it's usually because one or both of us is tired, and we're instantly apologetic.

Not this time.

I'm not going back.

"Okay, Elle," says my mom. "You win."

What?

Like that?

It's over?

But before I can say anything...

"You want the real reason?" She takes a step towards me. "I'll give you the real reason. I don't want you going to the concert without us. And we can't take you, so I'm sorry, you can't go. I'm sure Sam is perfectly responsible but no, you're not going with him. And your dad feels the same way."

I'm holding my cup but I have to put it down now, slowly, because my hand is shaking so much. She's never spoken like this to me, so coldly. It actually hurts.

And I don't know what to say. I count to ten, then I move away from her, putting the table between us.

"I get it," I tell her. "But you know what, you can't

stop me. I'm going, with or without your blessing, and unless you're prepared to bolt me into my room, there's nothing you can do about it."

I can also do cold. Clearly the apple doesn't fall far from the tree. And I can see that it hurts her too. But I charge on.

"What have I done to deserve being treated like this? I do everything you say; I don't put one foot out of place. And yet here you are, condemning me because of something that's your problem, not mine. It's not my problem that you're obsessed with me. It's not my problem that you spend your whole life worrying about me. That's your problem. I've got my own problems to deal with; don't put yours on me too."

I can tell that I've got to her; she's starting to tear up. I don't want this; it's horrible. I try to take a step back from where we're at.

"Mom, you're making such a big deal about this. It's only a concert."

Her voice is soft. "It is a big deal. And even a bigger deal because it's..."

She stopped.

"What, Mom? Because it's what?"

She's pushed me right back into the fray.

"Go on, Mom, say it. Because it's me. The freak."

"Elle, stop trying to be clever. And don't put words in my mouth. Yes, of course it's because it's you. It's you! My daughter! It's not about anybody else. I don't want anything happening to you."

She's tugging on a lock of her hair with one hand

173

and shaking her head. I know I shouldn't push her, but I can't help it. I'm getting angry too.

"You're not worried that something's going to happen to me, Mom. You're worried that I'm going to do something to myself."

Her head freezes mid shake.

"I can't believe you said that."

"You can't believe I said it out loud, you mean. That I said what you're thinking all the time. All the time!"

Her head's shaking again, but so is the rest of her body.

"Admit it, Mom. Admit it!"

Her voice is shaky too, but it's also deep.

"Don't you dare speak to me like that, Elle. You have no idea what I think about. But I'll let you know what I'm thinking right now. I'm thinking that any chance that you had of going to that concert is out the window."

"Oh, please," I shriek, startling myself. "I had no chance of going before I even asked you. You think that if you can control every minute of my waking hours, and my sleeping ones too, that you can control me. But you can't! You can't stop me from doing whatever I want to do!"

As soon as the words are out of my mouth, I want them back.

I want them unspoken.

I want them destroyed.

Because as much as I mean them, I don't mean them in the way that I know my mom is going to take them.

She's thinking that she can't stop me from doing whatever I want. Like killing myself.

Have you ever watched a tidal wave on TV? You know when one moment there's a powerful swelling of the sea, and the next thing it folds over on itself. That's what it is like watching my mom now. All her strength and bravado are wiped out.

But that's not what I mean. I don't mean that she can't stop me from killing myself. Because I will never do that. All I want her to know is that I have my own life and that she needs to let me live it.

But that's not what she's thinking.

What have I done?

# thirty-four

When I was about nine or ten, my elementary school was celebrating International Day of the Children and my mother was asked to give a brief presentation on the children of Africa. As usual, this made her mad. I was with her in the study when the phone call came through.

"Mr Tomkins," —that was my principal— "it will be my pleasure to talk to your students; I am unable, however, to describe the living conditions of every child in Africa, as my experience lies only in southern Africa, and as Africa has more countries than America has states, it would probably be impossible for anyone to do so."

After she put the phone down, she exploded.

"Bloody Americans! If I hear one more person say that they are going on holiday to Africa, or that they have come back from a business trip to Africa, or that they have an abiding connection to Africa, I'll scream!"

"Mom," I interrupted. "I am an American."

"Half an American. And you know better."

"Why do you get so angry when people talk about Africa?"

"It's not that; it's that they talk about Africa like it's one country; I bet you they'd only be able to name half a dozen countries there. Africa is an enormous continent, filled with diverse countries and people, with a myriad languages. You can't simply lump the whole lot under one title of 'Africa'. "

I'm sure I didn't get it then. But now I do. And more importantly, I get now what happened next.

My mom duly arrived for her talk at the school the following week. I was sitting near the front of the hall, with none of that teenage embarrassment we have today when we have to actually acknowledge that our parents exist. I was proud and excited. I don't remember exactly what she spoke about; what I do recall is that as I watched her on stage, I starting losing that feeling of excitement, and in its place came despair. The more I watched her, the harder it became to breathe. I only realized that I was crying when my teacher, sitting two seats down, leant across to ask what was wrong. I didn't know what was wrong. She asked if I thought I was going to faint; I nodded yes, not even knowing what that meant. I remember being led outside into the bright sunshine, and being told to sit on the steps with my head between my knees. And then I realized what was wrong. For some reason, watching my mother up there on the stage, it hit me for the first time that one day, she was going to die. And my dad was going to die. And everyone was going to die.

This was something that I unpacked with Miriam. And this was the reason why I had huge sympathy for my mom, and my dad. This had scared me, hell, petrified me in the real sense of the word—I was frozen solid at the thought of my parents dying. I guess it got easier as I got older because it stopped bothering me as much. But this is what bothers me now: I don't know how my parents can stand it, worried that every day could be my last.

Right now I don't have time to think anything through. I grab both my mom's arms, gabbling, "Sorry sorry sorry."

She's saying something under her breath. I lean in to hear her.

"It's all my fault, my fault, it's all my fault."

I shake her.

"Mom, this is not your fault. And I know it's not mine either. It's nobody's fault. It just is. And you've done everything—you and dad—to help me. I can't tell you how much better I am with knowing that you and dad are on my side. The therapy and the meds are one thing; knowing that you guys are always on my side is what makes the difference. But I know that I'm never going to completely have your trust."

My mom takes my hand and tries to say something but I don't let her.

"No, not that kind of trust. I know you trust me. But you don't trust what's inside of me. The part of me that you're worried that I don't have control over. I have tried to convince you that I do have control of it; that it's not like that, but I've hurt you and it's hard for you, I know all this. But you need to know that I will never do anything to myself. Feeling like being dead and actually doing something to cause this is so different."

Again, she tries to get a word in, but if I stop now, I don't know if I'll have the courage to start up again. I'm trying to think hard about the right words.

"No, you don't have to understand, you don't even have to try. Please let me have my say."

I swallow. She doesn't say anything in the pause.

"I don't want to kill myself. I will never kill myself."

We're both crying, silently.

"I've got a better chance of being killed by global warming than by doing that to myself." I hesitate. "Sorry, not sure what sort of comparison that is, but what I'm trying to say is that because sometimes I feel as if I shouldn't be here doesn't mean that I'm going to hurt myself. When I feel like that, it's like there's something else that gets to make that decision. Like fate. Or God. Or Allah. Or whoever or whatever. But it's not up to me.

"Yes, I get it that that goes against what I've said— that I have control over it. But whatever it is that makes me like this, doesn't want me to do it to myself. I want to be here, to be alive, with every inch of my body and soul. Does this make sense? What are you going to do when I tell you that I want to go to South Africa for a year after school? And after that when I go to college?

Mom, I'm making plans for my future. Don't laugh, but I want to study law too. And that at this rate, with Sylvia and Johnny sucking at it right now, I'm going to be the first one who gives you grandchildren! And I want to visit Germany sometime, and also go to Sri Lanka and Hungary. I want..."

My mom is still holding my hand in both of hers, and now she takes my other one too.

"It's okay, it's okay," she says, through her tears. "Oh my god, I think I get it. I think I get it."

She really starts to cry now, a groundswell of emotions that shakes her whole body and engulfs her and I can't hear her through her sobs. I take her in my arms, the child comforting the parent, and we cry together.

When she subsides back into just tears, she unwraps herself.

"There's nothing I can do," she says. "Is there?"

I shake my head.

"At least," I tell her, "nothing more than you're doing. You're doing everything. And don't stop. I still need you. But," I gulp, "you can't stop me."

She nods. "I know. I know now."

Her breath stutters as she tries to halt her tears.

"Have I? Have I been stopping you? From living your life?"

I know the answer to this one without even thinking about it.

"I wouldn't have a life without you. I don't only mean that you gave me life. I mean that my life—living with what I've got and what's inside me—would have been so much harder without you. On my bad days, you're the reason I can get out of bed. The reason I can live my life."

Now I'm the one overcome, and she's the one comforting me. And once I stop crying, which is after a really long time, I realize that she's been calm ever since she took me in her arms.

She's back. My mom's back.

"One thing," she says.

"Anything," I say, and right now, I really think I would do anything for her. Even not go to the concert.

"Not too soon with those grandchildren."

I laugh and cry.

"Speaking of Sam," she says.

"Oh my god, how did we get from grandchildren to Sam?!"

"Well. I've seen how you two look at each other."

"You've only seen him like twice in the past six years..."

"And both times you could cut through the sexual tension with a knife. What did Libby call it? A magical connection?"

Yuck. This is not a conversation I want to have with my mother.

"But seriously," she says. "I'm not saying yes, not saying no, not saying anything, not yet. Would you be happy going with Sam to the concert? Would you feel safe? I'm not going to even ask what Libby thinks—I bet she's been trying to convince you that hitching would be okay."

Um. Won't complicate that one with an answer.

"I am happy, Mom." And in more ways than one. "Sam's a good guy."

"I know he is. It's…This is a huge step for me."

"Well, let's do what Sam suggested," I say. "Have dinner with him and his parents. That might go some way to, I don't know, making you feel better."

"His mom will be there?" My mother seems puzzled.

"I don't know. I just assumed. Why, what's wrong with his mother?"

"Elle, Sam's mom doesn't live with them."

I stare at her. I didn't know that. My mom's already steaming ahead, though.

"It is a good idea. But I don't want Sam to think we don't trust him…"

"Mom, he knows you don't! Who in their right mind would trust a teenage guy with their teenage daughter?"

"There is that," she smiles.

"And that's why he suggested dinner. Then you get to reconnect with them, and we can take it from there."

"And Sam suggested this?"

"I told you. He's a good guy."

"And Libby's definitely going with you to the festival?"

"Wild horses, mom. Wild horses. But speak to Libby's mom—I don't mind you checking up on me. I am, after all, a teenager."

Her brow furrows. "Oh. We can't go to Sam's tonight. It's too late. Your dad won't be back from the city until much later. And I'm a wreck."

I sink down again.

"But Mom, then when? Tomorrow night will be too late. That's the night before the concert. You can't make me wait until then—that's not fair."

I pull away from her, but she won't let me go.

"Elle, don't, please don't. It'll be alright. Please give me one more day."

I'm too exhausted to argue. I know how much I've hurt her. So I give up. I still have no idea whether she'll let me go, but I know we've come so far and she's right. It will be alright.

"Please," she says.

She looks up at me from under her brow to see if this is okay. I nod. It's okay. We're okay.

# thirty-five

I'm still reading when I hear the front door open. It's after ten—another long day for my dad. I'm wired from the afternoon: From the fight with my mom and from the text message marathon I had after that with Sam. He's convinced that we're all good to go, so he's been making plans, and sending me links to route maps and the festival webpage and a funny site that lists the top ten things you must pack for a road trip, with number one being a sense of humor, and number ten toilet paper. We finally signed off late into the evening, and Sam's last words were, "Good night, sweet thing," which gave me butterflies in my stomach. I didn't say anything in return.

Libby sent me a text asking if I'd finally grown a backbone and told my parents that I was going to the concert, with or without their permission. I responded with a smiley face emoticon, and then ignored her other texts demanding to know what that meant.

I've taken my sleeping pill, but it doesn't seem to have touched sides, so I head downstairs. My dad is in the kitchen, standing next to a pot on the stove, watching it as it steams. He's slightly hunched over and the tail of his shirt is hanging out of his pants, but he's whistling quietly and tapping the fingers of one hand on the counter. I watch him for a moment. He's such a solid man—his shoulders are wide, his back is broad, his arms are thick. He's my headland; no matter how deep I am, I can always see him rising out from the water and guiding me home. I don't think there's anything he wouldn't do for me.

I haven't made a sound, but he must have sensed someone standing behind him because he turns his head. It isn't a sharp movement but his eyes are wide and keen. He blinks when he realizes it's me.

"Sheesh, Elle, what's with the creeping up on me?"

But he's smiling now and wraps me in his arms.

"How're you, honey bunny?"

"I'm good," I say. "And you?"

"I'm happy this day is over. Promise me that when you're all grown up, you won't turn into an ass."

"Dad!" I pretend to scold him. "Watch the language with the kids around."

He's opening the cocoa tin. "Want some?"

I shake my head.

"Mom rang me earlier," he says as he fills his mug with boiling water. "After you chatted."

I snort.

"Okay, okay, after your tear fest."

185

"That's more accurate," I say.

"And you're alright?"

I nod. I clench my fists, then release them.

"Dad?"

"Hmm," he says, through a mouthful of cocoa.

"Do you feel the same way? Like mom?"

"If you mean do I love you more than life itself, then yeah."

"Not that. I know that, you sentimental old man."

But now his eyes meet mine.

"I do. Feel the same way."

That's not what I want to hear. It's hard enough with one parent trembling on the precipice. I can't deal with two. And not my dad.

"But I don't feel it in the same way," he continues. "I worry. But I think somewhere along the line it became clear that I would have to let you go at some point. All parents do. Maybe your mom has just taken longer than normal."

I say, sulkily, "Because I'm not normal."

"You got that right."

I splutter.

"You're extraordinary," he says.

"And you're a twit," I say. But I don't mind so much. I know what he's trying to say.

"And your mom's extraordinary too."

"I know. We're fine. We're good."

"So I hear it's date night tomorrow night?"

"Excuse me?"

"We've got a date. With Sam."

186

"Oh, funny."

"Hope he's on his best behavior, because we're going to grill him."

"No, you're not!"

"No, we're not. A bit sensitive, are we?"

"Gimme a break, dad, it's been a rough day."

He hugs me. "And so it begins," he says into my hair.

"What?"

"Nothing," he says, but squeezes me even tighter with a bear-like growl.

"Shh, dad, I think mom's asleep."

"Your mother is definitely not asleep. The day—or rather night—she falls asleep before midnight is the day hell freezes over. Besides, she's still trying to finish The Illiad."

His eyes are on my face.

"You're sure you're okay?" he asks.

"Tired," I say.

"Me too. Time for bed, I think."

I follow him up the stairs, and he pauses at my bedroom door to turn and kiss me on the forehead. I wait until I hear him open his bedroom door; my mom's voice hums and my dad throws back at me: "Told you she wouldn't be asleep!"

It makes me smile.

# thirty-six

I'm shattered. The fight with my mom has taken it all out of me. My emotions are all over the place, tossed about in my river, which has risen during the afternoon and now has flecks of white foam on its surface. I sink back into it as I lie on my bed, but I feel in control. If I want to, I could get back up. I put on some music and while I'm listening to it, I try and sort out my thoughts.

I'm having supper at Sam's house tomorrow night.

I'm going to the concert. Maybe.

My parents are letting me go. Maybe.

I'm anxious. About supper at Sam's. About going to the concert. About my parents letting me go.

It's what I want. All of it. Maybe.

I focus on the music and at some point, I fall asleep.

Thursday

# thirty-seven

Today's a bad day.

Not a *really* bad day—I'm out of bed, and I'm moving, moving, moving. I'm not surprised—after yesterday's emotional overhaul and my late night, I thought I'd be in trouble today. But knowing this doesn't make it any easier, and I'm tearful. I watch myself in the mirror as I clean my teeth and brush my hair. I'm not telling my arms to move; they're doing it on their own. I'm frozen inside.

At school, I walk through the day, looking like an ordinary girl, talking like an ordinary girl, doing ordinary girl things. But it's so hard.

To make it worse, Libby's not here. She had told me yesterday, but it was only when I saw her empty spot next to mine in English that I remembered that she'd gone to some math conference. I don't know when she'll be back. I don't see Sam either. None of the seniors seem to be around today. We've all been summoned to the hall for the last period, and sitting on the excruciatingly uncomfortable plastic chairs, I dribble a couple of homeopathic anti-anxiety drops on my tongue and wait for them to do something to settle the unease. Something creaks above my head and I peer up—it's one of the big spotlights and the lighting guys must be moving it. I think, what would happen if the spotlight fell on me right now. Is it heavy enough to do some proper damage?

I'm glad I haven't seen Sam today because I don't want him to see me like this. Still, when I spot some seniors in the front of the hall, I find myself hunting for him. I catch Julie's eye by mistake; I've been avoiding her and Savannah, purposely sitting a row away from them because I'm not in the mood for their questions. Julie's mouthing something at me but I can't make it out, and she eventually gives up. The principal is up on the stage and she's talking about the importance of keeping up our studies during the vacation—yeah right, is muttered about the hall—and then she wishes us happy holidays. As she finishes, a drum beat starts up off stage and she smiles and says, "Hit it," as she walks off. Next thing, a horde of seniors from the front row scramble up and are leaping or cartwheeling or handspringing across the stage, and the school band enters from the wings, and the twenty or so students are doing a dreadful parody of a song that has been top of the YouTube hits for the last month or so, owing to the singular awfulness of the music video.

There is a ripple around me as students leap to their

feet, and the laughter in the hall is hysterical. I hardly notice, though, because Sam is on the stage. He's dressed in skinny jeans and a tank top and he is wearing a hideous wig that mimics a rocker from the 1980s. He doesn't look like Sam. But I know it is him the second he does a rather impressive handspring onto the stage. The boys in front of me stand up, and I'm on my feet, on my tiptoes, trying to see Sam. The girl next to me uses my shoulder to hoist herself onto her chair, then holds her hand out to me. I can see my smile reflected on her face—the vibe in the room is addictive. Then I'm on my chair and I find Sam again, and I'm clapping and laughing and singing along with the rest of the school until the students on stage perform a complicated routine that ends with all of them on their haunches, barking. The crowd goes wild. And through the mess of waving arms and clapping hands, I swear Sam finds me and looks right at me.

It's the last day of school before the Christmas break, so the entertainment in the hall signals the end of the day. Between the antics of the seniors and the anti-anxiety drops, my mood has improved radically. And, yeah, I guess seeing Sam might also have something to do with it. I take my time walking down to the parking lot, hoping to see him. No luck. My mom's already waiting for me, and as we drive off, I turn my head to watch the school buildings until they're out of sight.

I'm still a bit shaky around my mom and I'm wondering how she's feeling around me. This morning, she could tell it wasn't a good day and I could tell it bothered her more than usual. But it had taken a lot of effort to get ready for school so at some point I had switched off from monitoring her. Now, she asks me about my day and I smile, and tell her about the seniors' performance, finding the clip on my phone that's already made it onto YouTube to show her at the first stoplight we come to. She's laughing and I'm laughing and we're okay. I suddenly don't care about the festival. I don't care if I can't go. I only care that we're okay.

It's actually my mother who brings up the concert.

"So your dad played me some of Besiegung's songs," she says. "Dreadful stuff."

"An affront to the ears," I tease, quoting her from numerous other times when she's been exposed to our music. She's more of an easy-listening fan.

"You beast," she giggles.

We're nearly home before she says, "We had a long talk, your dad and I. Last night. Which explains these dark rings under my eyes. Well, it's either that or old age. And I'm sorry."

I don't interrupt—I can tell she's heading somewhere with this.

"You're right—it is my problem, not yours. So... so I want you to go. To the concert. With Libby. With Sam. In Sam's car."

What? I wasn't expecting this. But my mom hasn't finished yet.

"And you're right about something else. I can't stop you. And if I try to, you'll push me away and go on ahead without me anyway. I can let you live your life, or let you die living mine."

She jerks her head back. "God, that sounds dreadful; I didn't mean it to come out like that."

This time I do interrupt her.

"No, Mom, I know what you mean. Exactly what you mean. That's exactly it. That's it! You can't save me."

"No mother can save her child," she says slowly and sadly. "We will always try but we'll never succeed."

"But you will keep..." I swallow. "You will keep on trying?"

We pull into our driveway and I see that I've made her cry again.

"Always," she says.

And she's made me cry.

We lean into each other but not for long, because something occurs to me. I wipe my eyes.

"So we're not going to Sam's tonight?"

My mom pulls back.

"Oh, we are so going to Sam's tonight."

I turn to her.

"But, I thought you said I can go. To the concert, I mean."

"Yes, don't worry, yes, you're going. But that doesn't mean supper's off. I've already spoken to Sam's dad and it's all sorted. And if Sam doesn't pass the test, we might have to think again."

I can tell by her tone she's joking about that last point. At least, I hope so.

I don't even get through my front door before I'm texting Libby. Just three words.

It is on.

# thirty-eight

I don't hear back from Libby. Not via text, anyway. I'm still in the kitchen, making a sandwich when I hear a banging on the door. There is only one person who does that and, to be fair, she can't reach the doorbell from her chair. But she could knock.

I open the door and she wheelies up the one small step that leads into the hallway, and she's singing, "Töte das Biest!"

"You do know, Libby," I say, "that they have written a few other songs."

"So," she says. "Are you happy? Are you excited? We're going to Besiegung!"

"Of course I'm excited."

"Well, someone needs to tell your face that. You look like your dog died."

"Ah, Libby, I'm tired. It's been a mammoth battle. And I'm not entirely sure that I'm the victor."

"Of course you are! You have done the impossible. I

never thought you could—I'd already plotted our hitch-hiking route. Right now, I would hug you if I could!" she laughs.

I can't help myself. I smile back.

"You could hug me," I say. "I simply bend over like this and put my arms around…"

"Ew, what you doing? What I actually meant was I'd hug you if I felt like it. Which I don't."

But it's too late—I'm clutching her stiffened body and I'm laughing.

Libby tries to convince me that we need to go out and celebrate but I tell her that I've got therapy this afternoon. Usually, if I'd already been once in the week, I wouldn't go to my Thursday slot, but I told my mom that I wanted to go, partly because I know it will make her happy.

"Shouldn't you be getting ready for your date with Sam?" Libby puts an enormous amount of emphasis on the word 'date'.

"Since when is supper with two families a date? And I've told you, that's not what this is about. He's just a way to get to the concert."

"Yeah, a cute way."

"Ha, so you think he's cute? And he's really nice. Why don't you ask him out?" I swallow.

"Number one. I don't like Sam. Number two. Sam doesn't like me. Number three. Sam luuuurves you. But.

Number four. No boyfriends!"

This is accompanied by a thump of her wheelchair.

"C'mon Libby," I say. "That rule had its purpose, but don't you think it's time to move on?"

"No, actually, I don't." Her voice is cold. "Be honest."

"Honest?" I ask.

"Yeah. Honest to me and, more importantly, honest to yourself."

"And I guess you're now going to enlighten me about what I'm supposed to be honest about?"

She won't make eye contact with me.

"About how you feel about Sam. If you want to break the rule, then do it honestly. Don't try and put one on me."

I grab her armrests and shake her wheelchair.

"Libby, I don't want to date Sam. I don't want to date anyone. But that doesn't mean that you can't."

"Oh, whatever. But Sam? Jeez, Elle, even a blind man can see he has a huge crush on you. In a big way. And deny it all you like, you've got a crush on him too. And get your hands off my chair."

I lean back.

"I want you to be happy, Libby. And Sam too."

"You know what will make me happy? You freaking shutting up about this. And what'll make Sam happy? Only you."

# thirty-nine

We drop Libby at home before heading across to Miriam's office. My mom holds my hand as we walk in, which makes me feel about five years old, but it's not so bad. Miriam's in the reception office, and the way she embraces my mom signals to me that the two of them have had a conversation about all this. I'm glad. I know that Miriam would have gotten it out of me anyway, so it's going to make the session a lot easier.

"I'll be right here," says my mom, sitting down on a sofa and taking out a book that I know she won't read.

Miriam closes the door behind me and says, "Big day."

"Big week!" I say.

"Shall we celebrate with a cup of my finest tea?"

This is what I love about Miriam. She knows this has been a big step for both my mom and me.

"And then let's discuss why you're feeling as if this maybe hasn't been the best thing to happen."

This is what I don't love about Miriam. No small talk, no easing into the subject—let's go straight for the jugular.

"How do you know?"

"That you're not feeling great about this?"

"Duh," I say. Then, "Sorry."

"Because we've always known this would come at a price. We've talked about it. And the day has arrived, and I can see you're not having a good one."

I nod, and I'm sad.

"It's just that...that it's hurt my mom. And my dad. If this had never happened, we'd be carrying on as usual, happy families."

"Are you sure all of you would have been happy?"

"No. But at least they would be."

"Elle, you did the right thing. Yes, it's opened a can of worms, but rather see this, perhaps, as the worms being great composters, fertilizing the relationship between you and your parents."

I'm puzzled and a little grossed out.

"What exactly are the worms in that scenario?"

"Okay, okay, bad analogy," Miriam says, laughter in her voice. "But a good thing. And my advice for you is to try and move on from here. Don't dwell too much on what happened and on what was said; it's out there, and you are all ready to move on to the next step."

"And what's that?"

"Where do you think you need to go from here?"

A typical shrink response. I've called Miriam on this a couple of times—when she asks a question in answer to a question—but I know I was being otherwise then so I don't do it now.

"I guess we take it one day at a time. I mean, there are going to be other concerts. And I'm staying with Johnny for a bit right after Christmas. Maybe I'll visit Sylvia on spring break."

"That'll be nice. And what about your medication? Is it supporting you enough?"

Miriam's always spoken about antidepressants like that, as if they're only one tool in my arsenal. I don't think she wants me to forget that it's not the only thing that helps me.

I know that lots of teenagers are on antidepressants but I've read that some doctors are concerned about what these drugs do to the developing teenage brain. It seems they're designed for adult brains and no one is a hundred percent clear on what this does to teens. Also, from what I've read, no one's quite sure about how they actually work, which is not comforting. Miriam took two years to decide to put me on happy pills and then had to spend quite a lot of time convincing my parents that it was the right thing to do. At that point, I'd been following my new diet, running like I was training for the Olympics and keeping a journal to see if I could find any patterns to my sadness. My grief. But as I drew deeper into my teens, my bad days often turned into *really* bad days, and their frequency increased. Miriam had prepped me by slowly introducing the idea of antidepressants, giving me pamphlets to read and directing me to teen websites, but still, when she asked to see my parents and me together, I remember being anxious. Which you can't really help when you're already depressed.

I once read someone's account of being on meds, and what stood out for me was his description of how the antidepressants took his colors away; how he felt "emotionless and without thought" when he was on them. My bad days already took my colors from me; what would the meds do? That scared me. But I liked the idea of not thinking.

As it turned out, the meds actually returned my colors to me on a good day. And helped put my thoughts in order.

The thing I remember most clearly from that day that I started on the meds is Miriam emphasizing that antidepressants are not a quick fix—literally, they can take days or weeks to kick in—and that, ironically, when you first start taking them, or change to another type, that this can lead to suicidal tendencies—or in some cases, increased tendencies, in the first couple of months. I've been on antidepressants for a year now, and I don't remember exactly how I felt in those first few weeks of taking them. I can't even remember when they starting taking effect—it was such a gradual change in me, and it was only after five or six days in a row of good days that I understood they were working. I didn't tell my parents right away, or even Miriam, in case I jinxed it. I didn't quite think this through; they all would have been watching me like a hawk for any signs that things were going horribly wrong and would have easily spotted that they weren't. Miriam was the first one to bring it up, and when I told her how I was feeling, it felt like a confession. A weight off my mind.

Everything was going to be alright.

I—or whatever was doing this to me—slipped up every now and then and I would have a few bad days. And one or two *really* bad days. Mostly it was smooth sailing. But I know why Miriam is bringing up my medication now: It is a warning, however gentle, of the importance of keeping up with it regularly. I know this. Especially after the other incident.

# forty

About two months ago, I had a *really* bad day. Out of the blue, with no warning. It was different, too. This time I woke up at three in the morning with my heart swollen and pulsing in my chest. Images were flying across the lids of my closed eyes:

my Social Studies classroom,

Libby,

the lake from last year's vacation,

Mom,

Dad,

my bedroom,

the kitchen table,

Sylvia,

Johnny,

the hammock in the back yard,

the gas station we always stop at near school,

and more,

so many more.

I couldn't make them stop.

I wanted them to stop.

I felt ill. Like when you want to throw up. You get that heavy feeling in the back of your throat. Your saliva glands go into overtime. You try and swallow the heaviness back. You know that if you open your mouth, you'll vomit, so you can't even talk. Can't scream. But in my case, I was scared that if I opened my mouth, my river, which had encompassed my whole body, would flow into me and I'd drown. And I was scared that maybe I wanted this to happen.

It took all my strength to open my eyes, but the images were still there—like a slideshow of my life. I couldn't figure out if I was really awake, and I tried to sit up and one of my flailing arms hit my bedside lamp and it fell on me. I scrambled for its switch but the lamp was upside down and I couldn't find it right away.

Then the light came on.

I was awake.

The images were gone but I could still see them in negative when I blinked. I was damp and cold but I couldn't get out of bed. I tried to right the lamp onto the table next to the bed but my shaking hands sent it to the floor with a thump. I lay back down and tried my breathing techniques, tried to meditate, tried to stretch my limbs, tried and tried and tried, but I couldn't stop the tears and I couldn't stop the thoughts and I couldn't stop the images when I closed my eyes.

My mom woke earlier than usual that day, sensing, I guess, that something in the air was different. She found me in bed in the foetal position, my pillow drenched with the tears that had flowed for hours and hours, my body shaking with cold.

It was later that week that I decided to stop taking my meds. That *really* bad day had been followed by several bad days, and on the first good one I made my decision. I hated being imprisoned by the drugs that seemed to control me and decide when I would have good days or bad days. I didn't tell anyone, not even Libby, and it only took a few days before I started feeling the effects.

I flew into uncontrollable tantrums every time my parents said something I didn't agree with. I refused to go to school some days. I wouldn't hang out with Libby. I got called into the principal's office, and then the counsellor's, for swearing in class. I stopped eating; it seemed pointless. I was rude to Miriam in our sessions. I was tearful all the time, and so anxious that my nails left marks in my palms from clenching my fists. I knew things were going wrong but I didn't want to do anything about them.

These things didn't happen all on the same day. At first, there were small changes in my behaviour. But the red flags didn't go up until the changes became daily occurrences, and when my mother walked into the bathroom and found me trying to slit my wrists.

At least, that's what she thought I was trying to do. What she didn't know was that in my Health class that day we watched a DVD about cutting. As in cutting oneself. Also known as self-harming. Now that's a form of self-sabotage if I've ever heard one.

I was out of control that day; out of my mind. I was seething and silently raging against everything and everyone, trying to find something or someone to blame it on—to blame *me* on. During the DVD a number of reasons were given as to why cutters hurt themselves, but the one that got my attention was that some did it to find relief from the pain inside. I was fascinated, and wondered if anyone in our school did it, or in our class. And then I wondered what it felt like.

At home, I snuck a small, sharp paring knife upstairs with me, and when I heard my mom call out that she was shutting herself in her study for the afternoon to catch up on some work, I went to the bathroom and took off my shirt and sat in the tub.

Cutters usually make their marks where no one can see them, so I chose the inside of the top of my arm. I ran the blade lightly across my skin and then pressed it a little more firmly but this wasn't enough to break the skin. Then I pushed down hard and made a short, jagged incision. I jerked and gasped from the pain, and then actually giggled when I saw the tiny cut that all my effort had produced. There was a red line an inch long, with a drop of blood peeping from the top.

That's all I get? I thought. And that was freaking sore!

I squeezed the area where I had cut, and a bit more blood oozed out and onto my fingers. But really, I had done worse to myself while chopping carrots.

I couldn't imagine doing that again, and since all I

felt was pain and definitely no relief, I guessed you've got to cut yourself a lot deeper or a lot longer in order to get some sort of reaction.

To be honest, I was relieved. Relieved that it hadn't worked for me.

Maybe, I thought, I'm not that far gone. Maybe there's…

I interrupted my own thoughts—I suddenly got the feeling that there was someone on the other side of the bathroom door. Then the handle started to turn and I froze. Thank god I locked the door, which I don't usually do as I'm the only one who uses this bathroom. But the door opened.

What the hell?

At the same time as I was thinking, oh damn, it didn't lock properly, another part of my brain was going, this is going to be bad: I'm sitting in an empty bath in my bra and jeans, with a knife in my hand.

I dropped the knife and shielded it with my leg as my mom appeared in the doorway.

"Elle," she said, in a small voice. "What are you doing?"

But I had nothing. No way of explaining this away. Instead, I felt like giggling again.

"Elle. Oh my god, Elle! Is that blood? What's that? Is it blood?"

In two strides, my mother was at the tub. She grabbed my nearest arm and twisted it, and then the other arm. She was holding both of them and staring at my wrists, and then staring at me, with wild eyes.

"What have you done?"

She was confused, so sure about what I was doing but finding no evidence. Then she spotted the gash at the top of my arm.

"Is this... is this what you're doing? What are you doing? Oh god, Elle, what are you doing?"

She started to cry, still holding my arms as if she was offering them to me. And I was still sitting in the bath. I felt ill; my days, my weeks, of trying to cope on my own had caught up with me and I was breathless with fear: Fear of having to go on like this, fear of living like this, fear of how I had hurt my mother again.

I wanted to explain to her that this wasn't what she thought, but what did that mean anyway? Sorry, mom, this is a misunderstanding. I wasn't trying to slit my wrists; what I was actually doing was cutting a hole in my arm to see if that would make me whole again.

I think my mother thought I was in shock, and, looking back, maybe I was. She helped me out of the tub, blanching when she saw the knife I'd left behind. She gently manoeuvred my shirt over my head and tucked my arms carefully through the armholes. She found a plaster in the cabinet and stroked it over my wound. Then she guided me to my bedroom and sat me on the bed. She saw my phone on the desk, and she picked it up and texted somebody. My dad, most likely.

All this time I was silent. My mom opened my cupboard and shuffled through the shelf that contained my meds. She returned with two tablets—anxiety pills— and put them in my hand, passing me the glass of water that's always next to my bed.

But I shook my head.

"What's wrong?" she asked.

I cleared my throat.

"I don't take those anymore."

"What? But these are..." she turned back to the cupboard to read the tub she had taken them out of. "No, Elle, these are the right ones."

"No," I said. "I don't take them, I don't take any of them, anymore."

I was talking to the rug; I couldn't look her in the eye.

"You've stopped taking your meds." It wasn't a question.

"Okay," she said. "It's okay. I just need you to take these two tablets now, and then we'll talk about this. But you need to take these. Now."

I took them, and then curled up on my bed. I was done. My mom smoothed a blanket over me and then I felt the warmth of her body as she wrapped her arms around me and soothed me with her words.

"It's alright. Everything's alright. I love you, my darling Elle, and I'm not going to let anything happen to you."

She murmured her love for me until I fell asleep, exhausted from everything pent up inside me.

It took a lot for my mom to bounce back after that. I don't know why I couldn't tell her right away that I wasn't trying to kill myself. All three of us—me, my mom and my dad—were in Miriam's office the next morning, and only then did I manage to try and explain myself. Of course, none of them got it the first time round. I had to start all over again, from the very beginning, from why I stopped taking the meds and what happened after I watched the DVD on cutting, to why I wanted to cut myself and exactly what I was doing in the bathtub.

In the end, they all seemed to have accepted my explanation. I could tell my mom was still freaked out; Miriam and my dad were the ones who asked the questions. The only time my mom spoke was when I commented, "After all, I know my knowledge of anatomy is bad, but really? Mistaking my upper arm for my wrist?"

"That's not funny," my mother said, and not a facial muscle moved as she said that. When I had finished, Miriam asked my parents to wait outside. I got nervous. I felt like I had let Miriam down; she didn't make me feel like that, but if I were her, I'd feel let down. But she made me my cocoa, and told me she was thinking about getting a dog.

She asked me if I wanted to go back on the meds, and I said yes. And I meant it. Then she asked me if I still felt like self-harming, and I said no. And I meant that too.

So back on the antidepressants I went, but my mom and I didn't get back on track for a month. I was off school for 10 days—my mom wasn't taking any chances—and I was only allowed to see Libby. She sat next me at the kitchen table and examined my arm, mocking my poor attempt at cutting: "Jeez, Elle, can't you do anything right?" but I could tell she was thinking, how did I miss this? How did I not know she was going to do something?

My mom and dad were on eggshells around me, and it was during that time that I overheard them talking about me in their bedroom, when my mom had said, "Together." My mom increased her vigilance of me; sometimes I think when I went back to school, that she would drop me off, go around the block, and then park outside the school all day, just in case.

I knew I'd hurt everyone. I knew that I might not ever get their trust back again.

But here we are.

So I am confident today when I tell Miriam that all is well.

"In that case," she says, "the only thing left to do is to wish you good luck on your date tonight."

I groan and roll my eyes dramatically. "Not you too!"

In the car on the way home, I check my messages. There's a text from Sam: Listen, it says, don't you think it's a bit early in our relationship for us to be meeting each other's parents?

I know he's only kidding, but my heart beats anyway.

# forty-one

I don't remember my siblings living in our house—I guess I was too young to build up those memories—but what I do recall is neither of them being willing to give up their bedrooms once they left home.

Johnny had annexed the basement when he was a teenager, and Sylvia and I had adjacent rooms upstairs, with my parents' bedroom opposite ours. Johnny has relinquished some of the space in the basement for the stationary bike that never gets used and other pieces of retired equipment and furniture but his bed is still in there.

Sylvia removed the band posters from the walls in her room, but other than that, it's frozen in time from when she was 18. It's been promoted to the guest room, but never gets called anything other than Sylvia's room.

So I don't know what it's like living with other kids; as often as Johnny and Sylvia come to stay, it's still not the same as having a brother and sister on tap. I know Sam has two younger brothers, only a year or two below him. I wonder how this has shaped him. And I wonder how different I am from other kids who grew up with siblings. The way I remember Sam's brothers, it didn't sound like such a bad thing to be a sort-of only child. Back then, they seemed to spend much of their time shrieking around the house, hitting each other with baseball bats and throwing food at the wall.

No wonder Sam spent so much time at my home—it must have been heaven to him. What I don't remember is his mom leaving. I remember her, vaguely. But not her leaving.

When we pull up to Sam's house, I recognize it immediately. The front door opens and Sam's standing there; he must have been playing look-out. His dad comes up behind him; rather, I assume that it's his father as apart from a vague memory of his beard, I don't really remember him.

We all get out the car, and it's awkward. Like a first date with a guy. And his dad. Then my mom's hand is on my back; she's holding my father's hand, and the three of us walk up to the house.

The adults have taken their coffee into the den, and Sam and I are alone in the kitchen. The evening's gone well. I'm not sure how I pictured it all going but there was supper on the enclosed patio out back, some reminiscing about the neighborhood in the days before the expensive housing estates sprang up on the outskirts, a bottle of wine—possibly two, some serious talk about the government, and a lot of a laughter (mostly after the wine was finished).

Sam and I had both been quiet, sort of only speaking when spoken to. The adults didn't seem to notice our awkwardness, or perhaps they simply plowed through it.

But I'm feeling even more uncomfortable now that they're gone, and Sam and I are alone for the first time in the evening.

"Guess they're talking about the concert now," says Sam.

"I guess."

"It went well, I think. Supper, I mean."

"Oh, yeah, it did. I think my dad even called your dad 'bro' at some stage."

"What was *that* about?"

"I don't know. And I don't want to know!"

There's a photo of Sam and his brothers on the kitchen counter.

"Sam?"

"Anything," he says.

"What?" I'm confused. He's smiling at me and he's so cute.

"You want to ask me something. I'll answer anything."

If I held your hand, would you hold mine back? But what I really say is: "Um, your brothers. Where are they? They're not at school with us?"

The real question should be, where the hell is your mother? But I'm not brave enough to ask that.

"Thankfully not. My parents packed them off to Parklands when they hit high school."

Parklands is a private boarding academy an hour away from us, which focuses on maths and science and engineering. You've got to be pretty smart to get in there.

"So now you're wondering why I don't go there," says Sam.

"Oh, I *know* why you're not there."

He gives a skew grin, his brow frowning.

"No girls," I say.

He chuckles.

"Yeah, that too. But mainly because my parents knew I wouldn't get in. Obviously I got the cute genes; but Nick and Dale? They got the brains."

"Are you sure you got the cute genes?" I ask, picking up the photograph. "Because…"

"Oh, I'm sure," says Sam, turning on that smile as I look up at him.

Oh god. I look back down at the photo.

"So they're only here on weekends, then?"

"Yes! It's fantastic! I get the whole house to myself during the week. Of course, I'm ready to kill them by the time they head out on Sunday afternoon. But then, ahh, Sunday nights... The best night of the week."

I don't say anything to this. What I want to say is, can I spend Sunday nights with you? Can you make my Sunday nights go away?

I must have had a peculiar expression on my face, because Sam's asking, "Something wrong?"

Can I tell him? He wouldn't understand what I was talking about. But maybe he would.

"It's just," I say, "I've got a slightly different take on Sunday nights."

"How so?"

"Um. I guess you could say I feel lonely. Alone. I don't know. I don't like Sunday nights. I can't fall asleep. And it only happens on Sunday nights. If I could, I'd even give up Sundays so I could go straight through to Monday."

"You know that's strange, right? Giving up a day of the weekend?"

I nod.

"So Sunday nights must be pretty bad for you then."

I nod, slower now. I shouldn't have told him.

Sam isn't saying anything, then he speaks.

"Tell you what. This Sunday night, I'm going to call you."

"What?"

"I'm going to call you and we're going to talk. Or we can set up an IM chat or an online chat and we can, well, chat."

He stops, and the air goes shimmery, just for a moment.

"Then you won't be alone."

# forty-two

I'm sitting cross-legged on my bed, my duffel bag on the floor beside me, packed and ready to go. It turned really cold when we left Sam's house, so our goodbyes in the doorway were quick. Which was just as well, as I'd started to feel awkward with where the conversation had gone with Sam. I hadn't been in a hurry to go, but he was turning out to be a little too perfect for my liking, and I was worried that things were going to go weird again.

But we had been right; things had gone really well with our parents, and the trip was on.

So I'm texting Libby, and she's texting me back, and despite the sterility of text messages, I can feel her excitement. Or maybe it's that I can feel her excitement reflected in me. I know I have a lot to thank Libby for; her relentlessness over going to the festival—no matter how selfish her intentions—has taken me in a whole new direction, one in which I don't think I would have had the courage to take if it wasn't for her.

Despite my exhilaration, my sleeping tablet is taking effect, and I wriggle under my throw, and let my river take me.

*Friday*

# forty-three

Today's a bad day.

I don't realize it right away because today is not a usual day.

It's still dark when the alarm on my phone goes off at five in the morning. I don't usually set it—I keep such regular hours with my sleeping that I naturally wake up at more or less the same time every morning. But this is, of course, not every morning.

I had set my phone to "water music", hoping that the bubbling sounds of a river would soothe me awake. But no. My body is pounded out of sleep, and jerks. A split second later, my brain catches up and decodes the noise and my muscles relax. The bubbles wash over me and I float for a while. But not for long enough to doze off again and not for long enough to feel the bubbles competing with my river. It's high tide. I'm suddenly devastated. And not because I've become fully aware that it's a bad day, but because it's a bad day on this of all days. I can handle—just about—a bad day on an ordinary day. But I want today to be a good day.

I focus on what the day is going to be all about:

Libby,

the concert,

the road trip.

Sam.

But it's no good. It's still there. And if my mom finds out it's a bad day, I don't know what she'll do. No, I do know. There won't be any Libby, any road trip or any concert.

Or any Sam.

I'm holding my breath, so I let it out in a long stream. Then I'm moving,

moving,

moving.

I'm out of bed, fumbling for the light switch, and I'm swallowing a couple of anti-anxiety tablets and my antidepressant. My iPod is next to my bed, and I push in the buds and tap play. Besiegung rocks out and I take a deep breath, exhaling in a stream again. I want to go for a run, but Sam's going to be here in half an hour. I jog on the spot, wondering how long it will take to get my heart rate up.

Then my mom's tapping on my door and she peers around.

She smiles.

"What on earth are you doing?"

I can only just make out what she's saying, and I reply: "Uh, jogging."

She frowns and I pull out my ear buds.

"Why?" she asks.

Despite the wooziness in my head, I've got an answer.

"Limbering up. Remember, I'm gonna be in a car for hours this morning."

"Don't remind me."

She says it in an off-hand way, but I know she means it. I'm still jogging on the spot, but it's not working—I'm barely out of breath. I need to get away from my mom so that she doesn't suspect anything.

"I'm going to hit the shower," I say, and I jog out the room. There's a mirror on the wall in the passage and I glance at it as I pass, but I don't see my reflection. I stop; my heart doesn't. I take a step back and look into the mirror. I'm looking out at myself. I'm still here.

Half an hour later, I'm in the kitchen. My mom's pouring hot water into a flask and my dad's nursing a mug of coffee, looking out from bruised eyes and sallow cheeks. He's not a morning person. It takes a while—and a couple of caffeine infusions—for his features to fill out properly.

My mom seems to be able to exist on whatever sleep comes her way. She's a night owl, but she's as chirpy in the morning after four hours sleep as she is after ten. My dad's going to be easy to fool; my mom is a different story.

Even now, she's peering at me through the steam and asking, "Everything okay?"

I came up with a plan while I was in the shower: I

know that if I stop for even one moment, that I could lose it. So I'm following my same strategy of keeping moving, but with a little hyperactivity added to keep me from trying too hard. I'm opening the cupboards— "Where are the travelling mugs, Mom?"—and checking the contents of my bag—"Can I take your credit card in case of emergencies?"—and retying a shoelace— "Maybe I should change my shoes?" I talk right over her question, and then she's pointing to the shelf where the mugs are, and feeling for her wallet, and saying, "No, those shoes will be fine."

And then there's the flicker of lights on the windows, and Sam's here.

I hold my breath. My river sighs and draws back. I know that this is only temporary, but it will give me enough time to get going.

There's a knock on the door and my mother moves to open it, but I get there first.

Sam's wearing his usual uniform of jeans and hoodie. He obviously hasn't seen himself in a mirror yet because his hair is all mussed up and he's squinting through the bright light in the hallway and he looks impossibly cute.

"Hi," we both say at the same time. Sam turns away almost immediately to greet my mom, or maybe to avoid too much eye contact with me. My dad shakes his hand, and my parents walk me out into the darkness. It's freezing but we're all sort of standing around, shivering. My mom is drilling Sam about the route again, and gas stations, and frequent stops. My dad hugs me.

"Have fun. Not too much. But enough. Can I go

back to bed now?"

I squeeze him hard and kiss his cheek.

"Love you," I say.

Then my mom's got her arms around me and I'm close to tears. It's so dumb, and I know that it's mainly because of my bad day, but I'm also sure that even if it was a good day, I would be feeling a little like this. Surprisingly, my mom is quite calm. She does hold me for a moment longer than usual, but only a moment. Then she's giving Sam a quick hug; he's taken unawares and doesn't even get a chance to put out his arms and hug her back before she moves away to stand with my dad. Sam and I are both hovering by our car doors.

"Right, you two," says my mom. "In you get. And buckle up. And don't play your music too loudly—you won't be able to hear other cars..."

She fades out as we both slam our doors shut, but I hurriedly roll down my window.

"... phones on silent during the memorial but we'll check them regularly so phone anytime, anytime."

I nod, holding up my cellphone so she can see that I've got it, feeling like I have to do something to reassure her. I understand what she's doing now. She's doing what I do:

she's moving,

moving,

moving.

The only way she can hold on. So we're not that different after all.

Sam backs out the driveway and I wave goodbye. My

parents are standing together, my mom leaning into my dad, my dad holding her one hand in front of him with his other arm around her shoulders. I don't see them move away as we turn into the road, and I picture them frozen in time there and arriving back tonight to find them still there. Still together.

"So," says Sam.

"So," I say.

He risks a glance at me and I catch him doing it.

"Eyes front, soldier," I say.

"Yes, sir!"

He salutes with one hand.

"Hey, both hands on the steering wheel!"

He groans. "This is going to be a long day," he says, drawing out his words.

"Ha, just wait. You're going to have Libby to contend with too."

"Don't remind me. So there's no chance we can accidentally forget her?"

"Only if you don't value your life."

I stop.

Value your life.

Do I value my life?

If I want to be dead, if I don't want to exist, surely I don't value it?

But I do.

How does that work?

I shake it off. This is not the place for introspective contemplation.

Get a grip.

Our headlights skim the darkened house as we turn into Libby's driveway and, like a ripple effect, one window lights up, then another, and another, as someone moves through the rooms. Then the porch light comes on and Libby and her mom appear in the doorway.

For a change, Libby's mom is pushing her in the wheelchair down the ramp from the front door. Libby's got a small purse slung around her shoulder and her head is turned towards her mother.

Sam and I both get out the car.

"About time," says Libby, as a greeting.

I ignore her and say hello to her mom.

"And this is Sam, our personal driver," I say, and Sam walks around the car and shakes Libby's mom's hand.

"Alright, enough of the niceties, let's hit the road," says Libby.

She's wheeling herself to the car, and gesturing to Sam to pop the trunk. Then we both join her, and Sam leans down towards her.

"And what do you think you're doing?" she snaps at him. "You've got to at least take me out for a milkshake before you get to first base."

Sam looks at me. "A long day," he groans.

I scoop her up and put her on the seat.

"Is that all you're taking?" I ask, pointing at the purse.

"Got my phone, got my money. Anything else I do actually need, I'll bet you've got it anyway. No good doubling up on everything."

Sam folds up her chair into the trunk. Libby's mom squeezes my arm and says, "Good luck with this. Rather you than me..." But she's smiling and sticks her tongue out at Libby.

"Love you, angel child," she says, and blows her a kiss. Libby actually smiles at this, then rolls her eyes.

"C'mon, c'mon, dudes, we're not getting any younger."

# forty-four

We've been driving for over an hour, in relative silence, watching the darkness fade away and the horizon, washed of color, appear.

As soon as we took off, Libby rolled up her jacket as a pillow, lent against the door frame and said, "G'night." Sam spent the first quarter hour fiddling with the heating, then with the radio, then with his side mirror. I poured a cup of coffee from the flask my mom had packed, and we shared it, and I made certain that our fingers didn't touch during the hand-over. At one point he asked me to double check the route map on my phone, and later I made a comment about the number of cars on the road so early in the morning, and that was about it for small talk.

Just as well. All the activity of the morning so far has kept me going, but I'm still a little overwrought. I can't relax; being this close to Sam makes me nervous. I feel stupid. It's only Sam. He's just a friend. I don't want anything more. At least, I can't *want* to want anything more. It's too much. Libby's right. Boyfriends equal complications. But I can have a friend. A friend who's a boy. A boy whose knee is right next to mine. If I move my arm a couple of inches to the left, I could lay my hand on it…

Up ahead is a truck stop and Libby, who I think is still asleep, startles both Sam and me when she yells, "Breakfast!"

Sam pulls over and glides into a parking spot right outside the truck stop's diner. I'm glad we're taking a break—I need some activity.

I need to keep moving.

I get out the car and walk around to the trunk but Sam's got the same idea and we both reach it together and we're looking at each other and the air's shimmering and Sam takes a step towards me and I step towards him and this time I can't help myself and I reach out with one hand and touch his face with my fingertips. He doesn't move for a moment, then he reaches towards me.

No.

I snap myself out of it.

Complications.

No.

I pull away, breathing hard, and for once I'm thankful for Libby as her window rolls down and she says, "We haven't got all day, you know. Get me out of here."

I don't even glance at Sam as I help Libby into her

chair. She rolls herself to the door of the diner, but I have to help her wheelie up the small step at the entrance. I groan when I see the step. Here we go...

And Libby's off:

"Freaking losers," she says, loudly. "Elle, what's the name of this place? I'm reporting them. What?" she glares at a waitress who's staring at her. "Never seen a cripple before? What's with the step? And where's your table for the disabled? The one that will let me fit my wheelchair under it? Where? Where?"

The waitress is frozen, her mouth half open.

"Oh, you don't have one? There's a shocker. Give me your pen."

The waitress, on automatic, pulls the pen from her blouse pocket and hands it to her. Libby's spotted the name of the diner, flickering in neon lights above the counter, and copies it on to the back of her hand.

"You've been served," she says, jerking the pen back to the waitress. "Now, how about serving us?"

I haven't looked in Sam's direction once while this has been going on. I can't. I've been through this enough times with Libby, and every time it's as embarrassing, but at least I know it's coming. I don't want to see the expression on his face. He must be regretting getting involved with us.

But then he's standing in front of the waitress.

"Sorry about that," he says, "she hasn't had her coffee yet. Please could you get us three coffees"—I manage to shake my head and stutter, "Tea, please,"—"make that two coffees and one tea."

Libby's face is a sight. Her mouth is twisted in a snarl but she only gets as far as, "What the freaking..." when Sam grabs the handles of her chair and says to the waitress, loudly, over the sound of Libby cursing, "We'll seat ourselves."

I follow behind meekly.

Sam chooses the furthest table away from the counter and leaves Libby at the head of it, gesturing with an open palm for me to sit in the booth. I do so. I am in awe. And I'm wondering what sort of friendship Libby and I would have if I stood up to her all the time in the way that Sam just did. Probably no friendship at all. Not that I don't stand up to her; I have to pick my battles, though.

Sam walks back towards the counter, and then I look at Libby, who is still swearing. I interrupt her.

"Apoplectic," I say.

"What the hell?"

"Apoplectic. Overcome with anger. I've always loved reading that word, but I've never had an opportunity to use it myself. So thanks, Libby, for the opportunity."

She chucks her purse at me but I'm expecting it and I twist to one side. The purse lands on the table and I pick it up, handing it back to her.

"Want to try again?"

I can see the fire going out. But she's still angry, and snatches at one of the menus that Sam's returned with. She holds it up in front her.

Sam slides onto the bench opposite me and hands me a menu.

"Wow, I'm hungry. What looks good?"

As if nothing happened. I play along.

"Well, the croissant with jelly is tempting."

Sam's menu taps mine.

"You're kidding," he says. "Please tell me you're kidding."

"I'm kidding."

"Whew, that was a close one. Shall we try that again?"

"How about the greasy fry-up with everything?"

"That's more like it," he says, and he lifts his hand in the air.

I stare at it.

"Are you going to leave me hanging?" he asks.

"Are we living in the nineties?" I ask.

Sam obviously doesn't understand the ironic high five, and there's no chance I'm doing a real one.

He moves his hand to his head and scratches behind his ear.

"I'm going to pretend that didn't happen," he says.

"As am I," I say.

Libby thumps down her menu.

"I've had enough. You're freaks, both of you. Now where's my freaking coffee."

On cue, our waitress nervously approaches, then tries to put her tray down on the table by going around me so that she doesn't have to go anywhere near Libby. The mugs tip but she saves them from spilling just in time. She's still standing half behind me, her order book in her hand.

"Two number 5s, please," says Sam, "and for you, Libby?"

"Whatever," she says, and raises her menu in front of her face again.

"So make that three number 5s," says Sam.

Our meals are brought to us in record time—this waitress really wants us out of here. We eat in silence for a few minutes until Libby says, "Pass the ketchup," and Sam and I reach for it at the same time and our hands bump and our eyes meet and the air starts…

No.

I look away and bite my bottom lip so hard I'm amazed I don't break the skin.

I concentrate on my plate and eat every last bit before I chance a peek at Sam again. He seems to be doing the same thing—not taking his eyes off his plate—and is neatly organizing a mouthful onto his fork. But the moment's gone and I'm safe again.

I lean across the table and use my fork to pierce the last piece of bacon off his plate. I pop it in my mouth and grin at him. He doesn't grin back. In fact, he seems a little pissed. Disproportionately so for the crime of stealing his bacon.

"I can't believe you did that," he says.

"Did what?" I bat back innocently, although I'm feeling slightly nervous at his reaction.

"You know what you did."

"Enlighten me."

"You stole a piece of my bacon."

"And…?"

"Don't you know the theory of ratios?"

"Hmm, you mean like Euclid?"

"Okay, I'm impressed. Someone's been listening in math class. But no, not like Euclid. Sam's theory of ratios."

"You have your own theory? Now I'm impressed."

"Listen carefully. This might be the most important lesson you will ever learn. My theory of ratios is this: If you don't have the correct egg-bacon-hash brown-fried onion ratio, your breakfast will be ruined."

I'm relieved he isn't genuinely mad with me. But a bit concerned that he has his own breakfast ratio theory.

"You take your breakfast quite seriously," I say.

"Look, if you're going to eat that much unhealthy, fried junk, at least ensure that it will be the best meal you've ever eaten, especially since it could be your last."

That's one way of death I haven't considered. Death by over-eating. I squirm. Did I just make a death joke?

Sam's still on his breakfast rant.

"So by stealing that piece of bacon, you've put my ratios out of balance."

He starts stabbing at his food.

"One piece of egg."

Stab.

"One piece of hash brown."

Stab.

"One piece of onion."

Stab.

"One piece of—oh. No more bacon. Breakfast ruined."

Libby hasn't said anything up to this point. She's so hard to read; her facial expressions and her actions permanently scream "pissed off!", so it's difficult to know if she's still angry with me, or simply still angry with the world. Now she picks up a piece of her bacon with her fingers and lobs it over the table. It's a good shot—it lands in the middle of his plate.

"Happy now?" she asks.

"Oh my god, Libby! That's the nicest thing anyone's ever done for me. Well, the nicest thing you've ever done for me, that's for sure."

"Elle, for freak's sake, do we seriously have to spend another two hours with him?"

Well, at least she's talking to me.

"Don't forget the four hours back," Sam says.

Libby grenades another piece of bacon at him. This time it lands on his lap. Without missing a beat, he picks it up and tosses it back—aiming for her plate and getting his mark.

"No, thanks, Libby," he says. "More bacon would upset the ratios. And we wouldn't want that, now would we?"

The table shudders as Libby smacks her footrest against the bench.

"Freak," she says. "Come, Elle, let's roll."

I think that she's heading for the door, but then I see her take a left turn. Ah. I don't look at Sam; I just get up and follow her. If there isn't a disabled bathroom, Libby will need my help. This isn't as bad as it sounds—I only have to move her from her chair on to the toilet—the rest is up to her. I'm pleasantly surprised, though, to see a wheelchair sign over one of doors.

"Humph," says Libby. "One point for this place."

I use the regular bathroom, trying not to catch my own eyes when I wash up in the basin, worried about what I'll see there. I knock on Libby's door on the way out, and she swears at me. All good then. It's only now that it occurs to me: It *is* all good. I am good.

"You're really good to her," says Sam, as I slide back into the booth.

"Don't have much of a choice, do I?"

"Yeah, you do."

I shrug. "She gets me. It's not often that you find someone who gets you. She's a gigantic pain in the ass. But in her own warped way, she's good to me too."

"Really? I don't see it..."

"Oh, she never lets anybody see it. But it's there. You've just got to know where to look for it."

I swallow hard because what I'm thinking is that maybe if I got Sam to like Libby, things might develop between them so that Libby won't be alone one day, but what I'm feeling is something completely different. But I give it a go, anyway.

"And despite all appearances, she actually likes you. You should give her a chance. Get to know her better. And, after all, she is one of the hottest girls at school."

I know where I'm going with this, but by the

expression on Sam's face he doesn't.

"Besides," I continue, "we're more alike than you realize."

"Oh god, I hope not!"

Sam says this so loudly, it makes me laugh, even though I don't really feel like it.

"So you're crazy like her?" he asks.

"Depends what you mean by crazy."

"Well, I think there's two kinds of crazy. Crazy like, 'let's go to Vegas!' crazy, and crazy like, 'let's make a name for ourselves as serial killers' crazy."

"And which one do you think Libby is?"

"Both, I reckon."

"And me?" Although I suddenly realize that I don't want to know the answer.

"You," he says. "You I haven't been able to figure out yet."

"Figure what out?" Libby's back at the booth now.

"What kind of crazy Elle is."

"Oh, that's easy," she says. "The kind that spends every Thursday afternoon at...ow!"

My fork leaves three indents in her arm.

"Du bist eine Kuh!" I'm furious, but my words have distracted Sam from Libby's.

"I've been meaning to ask," says Sam. "What's with all the German? At least, I think it's German? I heard you two at school once."

He did? I wonder when. I wonder how long he's been noticing me.

"Elle didn't warn you? If you're going to a Besiegung

concert, you need to know that they only sing in Deutsch," Libby tells him.

"Yeah, I know that. I downloaded a couple of their songs."

Libby slaps her hands down on the table. "Illegally?"

"Hell, no." Sam holds his hands up, then looks at me. "I'm started to get worried about surviving this trip."

"I did warn you," I say.

"Actually," says Sam, "I'm looking forward to spending some time with the female of the species— we've been an all-male cast at home since my mom left."

Dinner at Sam's house last night had felt weird without a mother playing hostess, but I had been far too wound up to bring it up. Now, I blurt out, "When did she leave?"

"You know, when I was ten or so."

I blink. What? I thought my mom meant that Sam's mother had recently moved out. Not seven years ago. Not when I used to hang out with Sam.

All that time he spent at our house. He'd follow my mom everywhere. She always hugged him goodbye, and he never left without a box of biscuits or a pie wrapped in cellophane.

In my battle to get through a minute, an hour, a day, I don't seem to have the ability to take in what's happening around me all the time. Or rather, I don't have the capacity. I must have known that his mother had left—I would have heard from my parents, from neighbors, from kids at school, from Sam himself—but I didn't have the tools or space to contribute towards that.

But his mom left? That doesn't happen to boring middle-class families like ours who live in our neighborhood. People get divorced, sure, and the dad usually moves closer to the city, but I've never known anyone whose mom left.

It was Libby—shooting straight from the hip—who asked.

"What the freak do you mean your mom left? Like you woke up one morning and she was gone? Run off with the pool boy?"

Jeez Libby.

But Sam just laughed.

"Nothing as romantic as all that. She got offered a job in San Diego. Project manager for an IT business."

"She left you guys for a job?" Libby again.

"Her dream job."

"Okay, well that makes it better, then."

"I know, I know, it sounds as though it would be better if she had run off with the pool boy. But the truth is, her and my dad weren't happy with each other, and I think—I know—that it was a way out for her."

"So she left, never to be seen from again?"

"Yes. Unless of course you're not counting every year when we spend half the summer with her. And every other Christmas break. And the VOIP calls we make nearly every night to each other. And when she flies out to see us on our birthdays. And other special occasions. And…"

"You really had me going there with your poor little lost boy routine," says Libby. "So basically you're like every other deprived child of divorced parents. Boring."

She does a back reverse spin with a wheelie thrown in for good measure, and heads for the counter, tossing back, "I'll get the check."

Sam says to me. "Sorry, Elle, you're the one who must be bored. You've heard all of this a hundred times, right?"

I don't want to confess to him about how I'd never taken this in all those years ago. But I do want him to know how I feel.

"You must miss her so much."

He shrugs. "Oh, I think I've gotten used to it. My dad was a bit of a nightmare in the first year, but now it is—I don't know—normal, somehow. My mom still cries every time she sees us, and when she has to say goodbye. But I think they're both happier."

"And are you happy?"

I don't know where that came from. But I really want to know. His eyes are crinkling at me, but I'm careful not to meet them in case we go all weird again.

"It's just that," I stumble. "It's like I can't imagine a world where my mother isn't one of the first faces I see in the morning and the last one I see at night."

Where my mom isn't the one putting a Band Aid on my knee, making me pancakes with strawberry jelly on my birthday because she knows it's my favorite, watching my soccer games, taking me shopping for my first bra, making me laugh with her silly puns, watching Extreme Wipeout together and hating ourselves for enjoying it. Maybe it's different for boys. Maybe they get all that from their dads. But I couldn't imagine my life without my dad either.

Oh damn. It's not only my thoughts that have started wandering; my eyes have too, and now we're looking at each other.

"Elle," he whispers. "I miss her every day. Every single day."

Our eyes lock and it takes every ounce of my strength not to reach out across the table, take his face in my hands, and kiss him. I guess I'm stronger than Sam. Because that's exactly what he does to me.

# forty-five

We're back on the road again. Mercifully, Libby yelled, "Shotgun!" as we left the diner. I was relieved; I needed some space to think about what had happened so the back seat suited me fine.

We hit a flat stretch of road and Sam says, "I was going to make a soundtrack for our road trip, but then I decided that would be pre-empting it; kind of like making it a self-fulfilling prophecy."

"Dude," says Libby, "what the hell are you talking about?"

"OK, so if I got it wrong and I chose a bunch of songs that neither of you liked, you'd sulk"—he points a thumb at me on the backseat (huh? I thought), "and you'd bitch"—he points to Libby, who shrugs acceptingly. "It would be a very long drive.

"And," he says, holding up his hand as if he could see me as I open my mouth to object to the 'sulk' comment, "if I got the mood wrong, the trip could go horribly wrong. The car would break down, or we'd run out of gas, or you two would gang up on me, or…"

Libby groans. "Yes, we get it now, sorry I asked."

"So I have erred on the side of caution and made a compilation of around three hundred songs."

"Jeez, Louise," says Libby, "we could drive to Canada on those."

"I got country, I got blues, I got rock, I got rap, I got, well, I think you get the picture."

With that, he waves an electric blue flash drive around, and then plugs it into the radio console.

"If you don't like a song, we'll skip to the next one," he starts saying, but Libby breaks in.

"And then if we really like a song," she says, twisting around to me, "we can say"—she catches my eye and I get it right away and the two of us sing out— "Play it again, Sam!"

We collapse with laughter as Sam groans, "Yeah, like I've never heard that one before."

We've hummed and tapped and sung our way for over two hours, and have climbed the steep pass that's taken us to the top of Boulder Ridge. The music has done its usual magic with me, and my mood is definitely elevated, but I'm still treading water. Sam has tried to catch my eye in the mirror a couple of times but I managed to wriggle out of his line of sight to get some time on my own; some time to relive Sam's kiss over and over again. It wasn't a full-blown kiss, but it was firm and light at the same time; it was over in five seconds, but it was the best kiss I've ever had.

Right after, Sam appeared embarrassed, and said, "Sorry. I guess we'd better catch up to Libby."

I didn't—couldn't—say anything. I still don't know what to say, and luckily their time together in the front seats has actually got Sam and Libby talking, mostly about music. Now that we're nearly there, I'm feeling nervous; in the car, we can't do again what we did in the diner. But lost in the crowds at the concert, anything can happen.

We drive into the town on top of the pass.

"Okay, so we should be there in under an hour. We're cutting it fine so I hope it's easy to find," says Sam.

As he finishes speaking, a giant billboard slashed with blue and black and screaming in blood red "Fort Nottingham Festival" appears directly in front of us.

"Maybe that's a clue?" Libby says this, of course.

There's an arrow pointing to the right and Sam turns down the road, and almost immediately brakes sharply and pulls over.

"What the freak, Sam?"

We're in a gas station.

"You gals gonna thank me later. We'll fill up with gas now so we can hit the road as soon as Besiegung is finished and get you little ladies home before dark."

"What's with all the masculine talk? Do I need to hit you?" asks Libby.

Sam squirms. "Sorry, don't know what came over me. I think it's the small-town vibe."

I hand him the money my mom insisted we give him

for gas, and he steps out to work the pump.

Libby turns to me.

"Ich bin so gespannt," she says.

I consider this. You know, I am. I am excited. Oh my god, we're about to see Besiegung. I've been so caught up with Sam that I've forgotten the real reason why we're here.

I grab Libby's hand and we both shriek, "Töten das Tier!" and crack up.

It takes a few minutes until I'm in control of my laughter, and I smile as I see Sam heading to the booth to pay. Now he's standing at the counter, with his back to me. He looks good in a pair of jeans. He must have said something funny, because the clerk laughs as he gives Sam his change.

"Friend of yours?" I ask, when he gets back into the car.

He turns to me, confused.

"The clerk," I say. "You guys seemed to be getting on well."

"Jealous?"

"Ha!" But I blush a little. "Wondering what you said that made him laugh."

"Nope," he says. "I don't kiss and tell."

He winks at me and my blush spreads.

# forty-six

The last leg of our trip is a little slow-going as the road snakes across the plateau. Libby insists that we listen to nothing but Besiegung, "to acclimatize ourselves", she says, and she's trying to teach Sam some of the words, and he's not doing too badly. At one point, the three of us even do a pretty good job of harmonizing the chorus of one of the songs, and we all fall about laughing as it finishes, utterly high on the moment.

So I've got mixed emotions as we round a corner and draw up under a banner strewn across the road, featuring the same blood-red logo: Fort Nottingham Festival. It's awesome being so close to seeing Besiegung in the flesh, but my river is lapping against me as my anxiety levels rise. I know it's partly because the journey so far has been perfect, and fun, and chilled, and I got kissed... but I'm feeling like that when I get out of the car, the magic will be over.

I psych myself up.

It's all good.

All good.

All good.

With Libby's disability tickets opening up doors as usual, we're going to be heading to the VIP parking lot right behind the main stage. Getting there is another thing. The guard at the entrance gives us a map, whose directions indicate that we have to negotiate a grass road through the campsite, where some festivalgoers have ignored the yellow tape marking off the road, and corners of tents and ropes attached to pegs turn driving into a hazardous video game.

The festival started yesterday afternoon and clearly most of the campers had gone big last night, because there are not that many people around yet, and those that are, are walking zombie-like through the tent town in the direction of the stage that arises above us; distorted guitar sounds and a persistent base beat their siren call.

Someone's doing a soundcheck.

Libby's head turns sharply.

"It must be them. It's Besiegung. They're on first. It must be them!"

My heart palpitates. She's right. They could actually be up there right now.

Libby punches Sam on the shoulder.

"Drive, you freak, drive!"

"Libby," says Sam. "I'm not about to run someone over for you. I mean, I know we've bonded, but I'm not ready to kill someone for you."

He gets another punch for this and his groan of pain is for real—I know she got him in that soft, vulnerable spot under the shoulder blade.

"You been working out, or what?" he moans.

Libby ignores this.

"Drive!"

And we do, as I try and work out how I feel about Sam saying he's bonded with Libby.

Ten minutes later, and we arrive at the VIP parking ground. Sam flashes Libby's ticket at the security guard, and he opens the gate for us. We're in.

Sam parks as close to the entrance of the stage as he can, and he's out quickly and opens my door. Then he actually holds out his hand to me. I take it instinctively and step out the car. We're standing so close to one another that I have to lift my chin to see his face, and he still holds my hand and for a terrifying moment, I think he's going to kiss me again. Instead, I find myself being spun around and then he catches me in his arms and dips me, leaning over me and saying, "We're here!"

I feel faint; I'm not sure if it's from all the sudden movement after sitting in the car for so long, or if it's from being so near to Sam. Either way, he sees this in my face and hurriedly rights me up again.

"Sorry," he says. "I'm excited."

"Don't get out the house much, do you?"

It's not a great comment, but it's all I can come up with right now.

Meanwhile, Libby's glaring at us.

"Oh, please, you freaks, get a room already," she

growls. "But first, get me my chair!"

Despite the relatively early hour, there are already a hundred or so people mingling in the arena, some on their first beer of the day, while others are sitting cross-legged in the grass, eating burgers for breakfast.

Libby usually scores backstage tickets to watch from the wings, but this time she's forgone these to join the plebs in the arena.

Libby wheels herself in front of us and, with that, the sea parts. It isn't all voluntary by the innocent bystanders; Libby feels nothing to bash into a heel here or a shin bone there, but their reactions are always the same: At first angry, then embarrassed that they've got angry with a girl in a wheelchair, then taken aback at her appearance.

Sometimes she'll give them fair warning before she runs into them: "Crippled girl in a wheelchair coming thro-ough!"

Sam and I follow in her wake, side by side, so close that I can feel the warmth of his body as our arms scissor next to each other. I'm so aware of him; it's like we're moving as one.

Then our hands brush.

I don't react, but inside something that has been winding tighter and tighter suddenly lets go.

And then we touch again, but this time his fingers wind around mine. It's as if he has pulled me inside him.

On cue, Libby stretches around.

"What's happening back there?"

I pull away, right away, and wrap my arm around my

body, clutching my shoulder with my fingers that feel as if they've been scalded.

Sam answers. "Nothing much, your majesty, just basking in your reflected glory."

"Freak," she says.

Besiegung is mostly unknown in America; this is the first time they've played outside of Europe, so we weren't expecting a big crowd. Even so, the die-hards have already established a five-deep huddle at the front of the arena, but it's still loose enough for Libby to knock her way through. There's a fence running from left to right and between this and the stage stand several burly security guards. Libby wedges her chair right up against the fence and she uses her arms to move her body into a comfortable position, then the crowd around her closes ranks.

I see Sam has a plan as he grabs my hand—my heart races—and wedges his shoulder between the first row.

"Excuse me," he says loudly. "We're with the crippled girl."

I try to let go his hand at this, but he doesn't loosen his grip. As we reach the row behind Libby, she twists around and I can see that she heard Sam because she raises her arm, and the two of them slap palms.

"Nicely done," she says. "Finally," with raised eyebrows at me, "somebody gets how this works."

Sam's still got my hand in his but now I wrench it away.

"What?" he asks.

"I can't believe you've crossed over to the dark side,"

I say.

"Oh, but Elle, it's so much more fun over here," says Libby, her mouth smirking.

We're interrupted by a booming voice from the stage; a tall man dressed in a top hat and black cloak is yelling into his mic:

"Good morning, Fort Nottingham!"

The crowd goes wild. Well, more or less wild. It must still feel pretty early for most of them. But when I turn back, everyone's getting to their feet and making their way closer to the front, and in less than a minute, we're completely surrounded.

The MC makes some announcements and the tension builds up inside me, but I know this has got nothing to do with the fact that Sam's arm is pressed against me or that he's sliding his fingers between mine again. This all feels completely natural. What's unnatural is how fast my heart is beating when the MC finally screams through his mic, "Straight out of Germany, home to death metal, iiiiittttttt's Besiegung!"

The drummer must have been crouched down behind his kit, because suddenly he's sitting there and beating out a rhythm so loud and so fast the whole audience is jumping, including Sam and me. Libby's pounding her fists in the air, and then the rest of the band charges onto the stage and, as one, they all strike their guitars.

I scream. It's so loud that I give myself a bit of a scare, and I sneak an embarrassed glance at Sam, but he's not looking at me; he's fully focused on the stage.

Then I'm angry with myself; since when do I care what a boy thinks? I shake my head, let go of Sam's hand and throw myself into the music.

The first song is only instrumental, and then it flows seamlessly into the next one. We only need to hear the first few chords: It's Töte das Biest. Libby throws her head right back and howls. She keeps her head there and catches my eye. I grin wildly at her and she howls again. Then we're chanting along with the band: Töte das Biest, Töte das Biest, Töte das Biest… And the rest of the crowd is catching on... Töte das Biest, Töte das Biest, Töte das Biest until the song reaches its crescendo and now the crowd really does go wild. I cling to Libby's chair as I'm in danger of being swept away, and then I see Sam bend over Libby and in one movement she's on his shoulders and he's wrapped his arms around her legs and she's got one hand in his hair and the other one is punching the air and a pain strikes me across my chest as I see the two of them together, even though I know that Libby doesn't care whose shoulders she's on and I know that Sam's only doing this because he's Sam, but I care.

Damn.

The song's over and Sam's gently sliding Libby from his shoulders and back into her chair. Libby's on a high. "That," she yells over the sound of applause, "was the best time of my life!"

The lead singer, who is even more gorgeous in real life, is introducing the rest of the band, and then when he comes to himself, Libby and I both yell out, "Ich will dein Baby haben!"

He hears us, and says into his mic, "Jemand kann Deutsch."

We shriek like schoolgirls. Well, yes, we are schoolgirls, but too-cool-for-school girls.

Libby yells, "Wir haben es für Sie gelernt!"

He's spotted Libby now and comes closer.

"Na dann, dies ist für dich!"

And the band starts on one of their signature tunes, which is, naturally, anguished and groaning. The first part is slow and mournful, and the lead singer croons while staring into Libby's eyes. She's enthralled, and for that moment, I can see Libby as a teenage girl, with a crush on a singer, dating the high school football star and hanging out with her friends at a coffee shop. This saddens me suddenly and my mood drops a floor or two as the whole band joins in for the chorus. The crowd sways and I move unconsciously with them, my river ebbing and flowing. Then the beat picks up and the singer turns his back on Libby and the rest of us and urges the other band members on with his pounding fists. The crowd is in the air again but I'm still contemplating Libby, who catches me at it and smacks my arm. She mouths something over the music. I can't hear her so I lean in.

"It doesn't matter," she says, holding my eyes with hers, then she turns back to the stage, clapping her hands to the beat.

I'm not sure what she's talking about. It doesn't matter what she was trying to say? It doesn't matter that her moment with the band is over? It doesn't matter that she's paralyzed? Or that nothing matters?

But she's right. None of it does matter.

The band is back to its slow melancholy sound, so when Sam yells, "Gesundheit!" it startles both of Libby and me.

"What the hell?" says Libby.

"It's the only German I know," he says. "Oh, wait."

He cups his hands around his mouth and yells, "Kindergarten!"

I have to smile at him; he really is cute.

"Oh, oh," he says, "I've got one more! And it's brilliant... Creutzfeldt-Jakob!"

"A what now?" I laugh.

"Creutzfeldt-Jakob. Learnt about it in school. Creutzfeldt-Jakob disease is mad cow disease, named after the guys who invented—no, that's not right—I mean, who discovered mad cow."

"Hmm, so that's what I've got to look forward to as a senior?"

We're talking over Libby, loudly so that we can hear each other, and she smacks her hands between us.

"I'm still in the room, you know."

"Oh, we know," I say, rolling my eyes dramatically.

"Yeah, we know," says Sam, and he rolls his eyes too.

We're all laughing and the next song starts up and we're dancing.

An hour later, the singer announces the last song. It's as loud and furious as Töte das Biest, and I find myself being bumped away from Libby and back into the crowd. I'm dancing and singing along when I knock into Sam. I didn't know that he was there. I realize that he must have been standing there, watching me. He's not smiling; his expression's impassive and I can't read his face. I'm not moving either now, but we're both getting bumped from other dancers. Then I see his chest collapse; he must have been holding his breath. I look up at him and I know it's going to happen. His eyes pull me into him, and I pull him into me. And we're kissing and his hands are in my hair and I'm clutching at his shirt and we're kissing and his hands are touching my face and my hands are at his shoulders and we're kissing and he's lifting me up and my arms are around his neck and we're kissing,

and we're kissing,

and we're kissing.

I know that if I rose out of my body now and looked down upon us, that I'd see the whole crowd dancing and jumping and Sam and I would be in slow motion.

Kissing in slow motion.

Holding each other in slow motion.

Then in a clash of drums and a scream of guitars, the music suddenly ends, and there's a roar of applause. We're back in time with the throng around us, and we stop kissing. Our faces are still so close that the air can barely pass by, then Sam slowly slides me down his body until my feet are back on the ground. His arms are holding my waist and my hands are still around his neck.

"Hi," says Sam, but it comes out as a whisper. "I

mean, hi," he says, louder and deeper.

"Hi," I say, although I don't know if I even say it out loud.

I'm aware now that I'm being bumped by the guy next to me, who keeps elbowing me in the back as he claps. And Libby. Where's Libby? I drop my arms to my side and try and squirm away from Sam to find her. I see that we're sheltered from her by a couple of people, and suddenly I want to get back to her. But Sam hasn't let me go and draws his face down to me.

"This isn't over yet," he says. Then he lets me go, smiling.

Sam's sitting on the hood of his car nestling three bottles of water in his lap. He tosses one to each of us as we approach. I have just been with Libby to the bathroom area, if you can call it that. Although, of course, we get access to the disabled toilet built into a trailer, which is large and clean. Libby wanted to check her catheter bag; all that sitting on shoulders and bouncing about could have dislodged it, but all was good. Neither of us says much; Libby's still coming down from her high, and I'm still up there.

"It's very important to keep hydrated," Sam reads off a flyer he is holding. "And remember that too much alcohol can lead to a decrease in inhibitions, and you could find yourself in an uncomfortable or even dangerous situation."

"What the hell is that?" ask Libby.

"A safety guide for having fun at music festivals," says Sam. "Not sure how many people have read it, though—definitely saw some people with lowered inhibitions."

He looks right at me when he says this.

Libby wants to get something to eat before we leave so once again we follow her trail to the nearest tent that's selling food. Sam keeps trying to catch my hand and I keep slapping him away. But playfully. I've come to a decision. This is a one-time thing. This will not happen again. What happens at the festival stays at the festival. But while we're still here… I let him catch my hand.

My head knocks against the car window and I jerk up, blinking in the light. Sam takes one hand off the wheel and puts it on my knee.

"It's okay. You fell asleep."

He removes his hand, but I can still feel the imprint of his fingers on my leg. I can't believe I fell asleep. I can't believe I fell asleep when I only have a few hours left with Sam. My neck is stiff and I'm groggy. And my river's back.

I twist around to see Libby. Her head rests against the window and her eyes are closed. She looks peaceful. She looks beautiful. I wonder what I look like when I'm asleep. What Sam thinks of me when I sleep.

"She still sleeping?" asks Sam quietly.

"Yip," I say, as I turn back to him. He reaches his hand over to me again, glancing up for a second to find my hand, and then he takes it in his.

"Free at last," he whispers.

I curl around towards him, pulling our hands to rest on my stomach, and I watch him as he drives.

"Stop that," he says.

"What?" I say.

"Stop looking at me."

"But I like looking at you."

"Yes, but I can't look at you, so it's unfair."

"Okay," I say. "I'll close my eyes."

But I don't.

After a few moments, he says, "Stop it."

"What?"

"Stop looking at me."

So I coil in the opposite direction, taking his hand with me.

"Ow," he mutters. "Elle, I don't think my hand is supposed to twist like that."

Embarrassed, I let go.

"Sorry, sorry."

He looks at me. I look back. He looks at the road, then back at me. Then we're both leaning in and we kiss. A light touch, and he's looking at the road again, but I can't help running my fingers across my lips.

"Okay, talk to me," Sam says.

"About what?"

"Anything. No, not anything. Nothing that will make

me want to kiss you again. This is getting dangerous. No driving and kissing. So tell me a dirty joke—no, no, not a dirty joke—I mean like a joke that is disgusting, that'll make me want to, I don't know, throw up. That'll take my mind off things. Off you."

My heart flips. Then I hear Libby stir.

No.

I want more time with him.

Alone.

But Libby's awake.

"Where the hell are we?"

She peers out the window.

"Oh, still the middle of freaking nowhere. And what's up with those clouds?"

Sam and I both bend to see out her side. A formation of birds is outlined against the sky, then they disappear in front of a wall of dark clouds. A flash of light highlights them and they're gone again.

"Was that lightning?" I ask.

"Damn freaking right it was," says Libby. "And those clouds are coming our way."

For a second I can see us holed up in a diner, waiting out the storm, Sam wrapping me in his arms every time I jump at the lightning flashes and laughing at me. Libby… well, I don't actually see Libby in this wishful thinking.

But the signs for the Boulder Rise pass loom up ahead, and there's nowhere to stop until we get to the bottom. At least we'll have to go slower now, which means more time with Sam. As we turn onto the pass, the sky splits and light lashes the car, followed by a drum roll that seems to go on and on. Then the rain comes down, hard.

Sam's shoulders hunch as he drives, and Libby and I are both quiet. Two cars appear out of nowhere on the opposite side of the road, the rain blurring their outlines, and as quickly they are past us. The rain comes down harder.

It is difficult to tell where the road is and where it is going, and being on the pass means that there is no shoulder to pull over onto—the mountain rises above us on the one side, and drops below on the other. Sam almost tiptoes the car around the bends, hazards flashing in the hope that if we can't see another car, perhaps it can see us. Then, with a suddenness that surprises us, the rain withdraws. A minute later, Sam unclenches his body and blows out a rush of breath.

"I'm not going to lie," he says. "That was scary. I thought for sure that was over for us."

Libby touches my shoulder. "So close," she murmurs, and I turn sideways and whack her arm.

"Sam," I say. "I think you just saved our lives."

I'm still half-turned so I can see Libby is staring out the window at the fall of rocks below us. I reach across and put my hand on Sam's shoulder. His head crooks and I feel his warm cheek on my skin. Libby shifts in her seat and I lift my arm quickly in a fake stretch.

"Whew, I could do with some air," I say, turning to her, but her eyes are narrow and suspicious. But I don't think I care. I catch her eye.

"A good day," I say, softly.

She nods and holds my eye, then turns back to her window.

The deluge has effectively put an end to the daylight, although the clouds are paler now, as if shocked by the fierceness of the storm.

The last mile of the pass arcs before us. The headlamps are bouncing light off the road, which is streaming with water from the downpour that came before. At the final turn, the back wheels lose their grip and there's a collective intake of breath as the tail of the car slides towards the rock face. But Sam's on form, and corrects the wheel slightly, and we're back on track.

"Freaking hell," says Libby. "Get us off this road."

"As you wish, m'lady," says Sam, sidling up to the stop sign that indicates we're finally at the bottom of the pass. He turns around so he can see both Libby and me and raises his hands in the air.

"After that sterling piece of driving, surely neither of you can deny me an up high…"

He breaks off, staring behind Libby.

"Jeez, I don't think that…"

When the truck hits us from behind, our car is slammed into the intersection. The crossroad is quiet and there's nothing in our way. Nothing to hamper the car skimming along the surface, the wheels helpless against the water-logged road. Nothing to stop it smacking into the curb on the opposite side, pitching it onto its back, slamming it into something hard and solid.

Someone is screaming the whole time this is happening, but as we flip over and hit the ground with a clash of metal, the screaming stops. I can't be sure if I was the one screaming or not. All I can hear now is someone's rasping breath. I hold my own breath—it's not me. I try and get my bearings, but something's not quite right with my vision—everything in front of my eyes seems bruised and purple.

"Libby," I say. Nothing. Something hurts deep inside me.

"Sam?" Nothing. That hurt again.

And the sound of that ragged breathing.

I realize that I'm sort of upside down. I've slipped through part of my buckle at the top but the bottom strap is pressing painfully across my stomach. I feel for the clip. I can't push the button in; the strap is too taut. My feet find something solid and I brace myself up. Oh god, that's sore. But the clip opens and it snaps me onto the floor. No, not the floor. The roof. I'm crouching on the ceiling of the car, and I'm burning up inside. I gently run my hands over my torso; nothing hurts until I press down on my belly. I want to shriek but the pain has taken my breath away. I huddle for a moment. The pain subsides to an ache. My eyesight seems better now; I can see Sam hanging next to me, his arms and legs rag-dolled below his body.

"Sam," I say. "Sam!"

It hurts to talk, and it hurts even worse when there's only silence in return. But I can see his chest rise and fall; the breathing is coming from him. I move gingerly, not knowing where the pain inside me is, so that I can see between the seats. Libby's hanging at a strange angle; she must have been flung forward and down—her legs are trapped under my seat.

I touch her hand and it moves.

"Libby," I say.

"Mmm," she says.

Oh thank god.

"Libby, I think you're stuck. I'm going to try and get out the car and then come and get you."

She doesn't say anything. I pull the door handle and nearly cry when the door won't open. I try again, and this time it moves. I crawl out. It hurts so badly that now I do start to cry. Only little sobs of breath, as even crying hurts. I'm sitting on my haunches; I can see the truck in the middle of the road and through the cracked windshield I can see an arm, but it's motionless.

"Help," I croak.

I try a little louder.

"Help!"

I have barely raised my voice, but pain wracks my body and starts the sobbing again. I close my eyes and find my river and focus on it. It's rising and I will it higher and higher, and the pain diminishes. I open my eyes and shuffle to Libby's door. The first tug only results in agony, but then I see a hand on the window. It's pushing. So I yank again, and the door opens.

"Glad you could make it," Libby says, then closes her eyes.

"Libby," I whisper, knowing that any louder will hurt.

"Still here," she says. "I feel really strange."

There's blood on her face, but the thing that still worries me is her legs. They're twisted and buckled, and I'm sure they're both broken.

"Your legs."

"I know," she says. "You'd think I wouldn't be able to feel anything, but freaking hell, I'm feeling something somewhere. Something bad."

I reach into the car, swallowing the pain, and feel underneath the seat. One of Libby's feet is lying free, but the other is wedged. I take hold of her ankle and try to wriggle her foot out. It moves a little, but then holds fast. I don't know what to do. I sit there for a minute.

A phone. We need help. I can phone!

"Libby, where's your phone? We need to phone."

"What's that smell?" asks Libby.

"No," I say, confused. "Where's your phone?"

"It's smoke. Elle, I can smell smoke."

Now I get it. And now I can smell it too. I lean back slowly so I can see outside the car but I can't make out much in the gloom. Then I see a lick of flame.

"Elle," says Libby, her voice very steady. "Elle, I need you to get me out of here.

Now.

Right now.

Get me out now."

It's her voice—calm and unfaltering—that sets off an alarm in me. Libby is scared. I take her ankle in both my hands and say, "Grab your left leg and on three, pull."

She nods.

"One, two, three."

The pain that's been rolling around inside my torso suddenly solidifies, then explodes. I hear a sound come from deep inside me—but it can't be me creating this roar, this bellow, this howl. I'm doubled over and I can't move, and then I feel arms around me and I'm floating up and I see Sam's eyes and I see darkness.

I hear a strange voice first.

"They're on their way already. I called 911 as soon as I saw your car."

Then Libby's voice. "What's wrong with her? There's no blood or anything."

Sam. "Maybe she hit her head too."

There's a woman leaning over me and when she sees my eyes are open, she says, from very far away, "Honey, where do you hurt?"

Everywhere.

But wait.

Nowhere.

The pain is gone.

And I know why. I'm completely submerged in my river. It's clear and it's warm and I'm cocooned in its waters.

The woman pulls up my shirt and I hear her gasp. It

occurs to me when I lift my head that I must be lying down. I can only hold up my head for a few seconds, enough time to see my stomach dyed purple.

"Shh," says Sam, his fingers stroking my forehead. I lie back down, knowing now that my head is resting on Sam's lap. I can see his face above mine—although it doesn't seem that close— and I smile; at least, I think that's what I'm doing. I must have done something right because now he's smiling too. His face seems a bit distorted from the red lump on his forehead, but he still looks gorgeous.

"I think she's bleeding inside," the woman says. "You know, internally."

"That's not good," says Libby. "Is it?"

Her voice is coming from next to me, so I turn my head. She also appears to be lying down, and the blood that had been dripping down her face is now smeared across it—she looks like some kind of Amazon warrior. She'd like that. I wish I could tell her this, but I don't seem able to speak.

"You got me out," she says, her voice sounding muggy.

"The car was filling up with smoke when I pulled over," says the woman. "I sprayed the engine with my car fire extinguisher—it's really small but I think it stopped whatever was burning."

Libby's hand finds mine and I squeeze it. She doesn't let go. I smile at her; again, it feels weird, as if my muscles have forgotten how to, but she gives me half a wince, half a smile back, so I guess maybe she's having the same problem I have.

I feel happy.

What a peculiar thought to be having at this moment. But I'm right. I think I am happy. Like blissfully content. I think what I am experiencing is pure happiness.

So this is what it's like.

It's beautiful.

I'm here at last.

I feel... I feel triumphant.

There's an undercurrent beneath my river, and I know that if I descend a little bit lower, it will take me away.

Libby's hand suddenly tightens around mine. I look down and see that my hand has fallen limp at my side. I look at her.

"Don't go," she says, although her voice is so muffled that I think I might be lip-reading.

Sam's fingers are lapping through my hair and I sink down a little further.

Happy, I think to myself. Maybe I manage to say it out loud, because Libby squeezes my hand again, and Sam's lips brush my forehead.

I'm swathed now in layers of warm, silky water.

I take a breath.

And then I let go.

*"And fate? No one alive has ever escaped it, neither brave man nor coward, I tell you—it's born with us the day we are born."*
— Homer, The Iliad

# Acknowledgements

To my beta readers: Lolly, Donna and Yves - the best birthday present ever! To Cate, for understanding what a drag smalltalk can be, for being able to speak German, and for her vehement opposition to the cover everyone else liked. To Rachel Morgan, for all her advice and guidance and patience! To my parents, for filling my room with books. And to Chris, for reading to me when I can't fall asleep.

# About the Author

Philippa Cameron is the head of a media center and a teacher of information and digital literacy. In a previous life, she was a journalist and a lecturer. She lives with her husband, two daughters and two Guinea pigs who appeared in her home without her consent. The Guinea pigs, not her husband and daughters. She also lives with depression, but she doesn't let that get her down.

www.philippa-cameron.com
facebook.com/philippacameronwriter
twitter.com/writerphilippa

Look out for *So We Beat On*, a free Elements novella to accompany *The Day We Are Born*.

The next book in the Elements series,
*Every Move I Have Made*, will be out in 2015!

Made in the
USA
Monee, IL